# Reproduction

# Reproduction

A Novel

## Louisa Hall

**ecco**

*An Imprint of* HarperCollins*Publishers*

REPRODUCTION. Copyright © 2023 by Louisa Hall. All rights reserved. Printed in the United States of America. No part of this book may be used or reproduced in any manner whatsoever without written permission except in the case of brief quotations embodied in critical articles and reviews. For information, address HarperCollins Publishers, 195 Broadway, New York, NY 10007.

HarperCollins books may be purchased for educational, business, or sales promotional use. For information, please email the Special Markets Department at SPsales@harpercollins.com.

Ecco® and HarperCollins® are trademarks of HarperCollins Publishers.

FIRST EDITION

Library of Congress Cataloging-in-Publication Data has been applied for.

ISBN 978-0-06-328362-6

23 24 25 26 27  LBC  5 4 3 2 1

What I ask of you is reasonable and moderate;
I demand a creature . . .

> —THE MONSTER, in Mary Shelley's *Frankenstein*


when Something drops onto her toes one night
she calls it a fox
but she feeds it.

> —LUCILLE CLIFTON, "my dream about the second coming"

# Contents

✕

# Reproduction

# Conception

2018

I BEGAN WORK ON A NOVEL ABOUT MARY SHELLEY IN 2018, when I was pregnant for the first time. It was a few months after my husband and I had moved from New York to a town in Montana, where the weather was getting colder and the days were getting darker. It was a strange time in the country, and a strange time in my own life. Perhaps because of the move, or perhaps because of the pregnancy, I had many unusual dreams. I often woke up in an odd, groggy state, in which it was difficult for me to focus on Mary Shelley.

Still, however, parts of her story detached themselves from the page and clung to my life. The fact, for instance, that in her later years she recalled that *Frankenstein* was written in the aftermath of a "waking dream": a "pale student" kneeling beside a creature he'd sewn together. The vision terrified her, she said, so absolutely that she couldn't shake it all through that strange, gloomy summer, the summer of 1816, the year after the fall of the Napoleonic empire, when ash from the volcanic eruption at Mount Tambora had blotted out the sun's light.

The ash from that volcano remained in the atmosphere for three years, darkening the sky, so that on several continents the warm growing season never arrived. It caused famines and a cholera pandemic that killed tens of millions of people. In Italy, at Lord Byron's villa on the banks of Lake Geneva, where Mary Shelley was staying with Percy and her stepsister, Claire, it caused a summer of uninterrupted darkness.

All summer, she and Percy and Claire and Lord Byron spent their days indoors, with candles lit, reading ghost stories and morbid poems until Byron challenged them all to come up with their own frightening tales. For weeks, Mary tried, but she couldn't come up with a story. She was mortified by her failure. It was only in the days after that waking dream that she conceived of *Frankenstein*.

That summer, she was nineteen. She had recently given birth to a child. It was her second. The first baby, a girl, came when she was seventeen. That baby was two months premature. She lived for two weeks and died before the end of the winter.

"My dearest Hogg my baby is dead," she wrote in a letter to a friend:

Will you come see me as soon as you can. I wish
to see you—it was perfectly well when I went to
bed—I awoke in the night to give it suck it appeared
to be sleeping so quietly that I would not awake it.
It was dead then, but we did not find that out till
morning—from its appearance it evidently died
of convulsions—Will you come—you are so calm
a creature & Shelley is afraid of a fever from the
milk—for I am no longer a mother now.

She reconceived a few months later, and gave birth the following spring, and it was that summer that she and Percy and Claire went to Lake Geneva to visit Lord Byron, and Mary conceived of *Frankenstein*, as well as a series of travelogues about their journey through France and Italy.

IN THE WEEKS before we moved to Montana, where I'd taken a job teaching writing, I packed up the apartment while my husband was at work. That summer, the heat never broke. We'd finally found an air conditioner to put up in the bedroom, but the rest of the apartment was dusty and hot. In between packing boxes, I often took breaks and stood by the window to look out on the street where we'd lived for one year.

That year: it had been a happy time in my life. The apartment was infested with mice, but it had large bay windows facing out to the street. They were flooded with sunlight in the afternoon, full of gently stirring sycamore leaves, so that at certain hours of the day, the shadows of the leaves played across pools of light on the walls in a way that made it seem as if we lived underwater.

It's true that it was a grim time in the country at large. Every day, it seemed, there was a new mass shooting; every month, a Muslim ban was instated or overturned. And meanwhile, it was clear that the weather was changing. That fall was so warm the leaves on the ginkgo trees didn't change. They clung greenly on all through October and November until, one night in December, we had a rainstorm. The next morning, the gutters were clogged with little green fans.

By then, the forest fires in California were already burning. They were, at that time, the worst fires in California's history. The flames raged behind my parents' house and crept down the side of the mountain where they lived, and a firefighter died on their street, trying to keep the blaze from consuming the houses.

In January, my parents were evacuated. They gathered the dog and their most important possessions and moved to a place called the Seashell Motel. When they finally returned to their house, a heavy rain fell, and because there were no longer any trees to hold down the dirt on the mountain, mudslides began gathering strength, running through their neighborhood and eventually tearing away most of the houses that remained on their street. For some reason, however, their house remained standing, so that if they had not evacuated once again to the Seashell Motel, they could have sat by the large windows in their living room, facing the road, watching cars float by and then houses, which is what their neighbors—a widowed man and his two children—did from the roof. They lived a bit farther down the hill, and for some reason that part of the street was not given an evacuation order, so when water began to rise in their house, they climbed up to the roof, and remained there, holding one another, until one of the children—the daughter—was swept away and never recovered.

SOMETIMES, DURING THAT happy winter, I spoke to my mother on the phone. In general, she was remarkably cheerful, though her street was now lined with the empty concrete holes of what used to be basements. When they received their third evacuation order, however, she told me she was considering resisting it. "Sometimes," she said, "you just want to stay where you are and watch the rain wash it all away."

I listened, sort of, but I was so happy. I lived in a sunny apartment with a man I'd fallen in love with. I'd wound my life back together again, after the years when it had come unraveled. I was so happy I couldn't even read novels, with all their obsessing over the minutiae of suffering. Instead, I read children's books by Tove Jansson.

Sometimes, from California, my mother sent me articles about global warming. I tried not to read them. I read, instead, about the Moomin family rebuilding their little blue house in a new valley, and Moominpappa writing his memoirs, and Moominmamma and her blue pears, and Moomintroll setting off to climb Lonely Mountain.

When I wasn't reading, I took long walks. It was spring. A rainy March had washed the sky clear, and now everything was almost unbearably bright. On Eastern Parkway, I walked under the pale green blossoms of the golden elms, tumbling cartoonishly above me. On the street, little children on their way home from school ran before me happily. When I got home, I spent the afternoons writing poems about Moomins in a little red notebook, moving around the apartment, competing with the dog for the best patches of sunlight. When my husband came home from work, the dog and I both ran to the door, smiling like idiots.

THIS IS WHAT I remembered when I stood at the window, looking out on the street. The dog trembled at my feet. He hated boxes; he never got used to them, though, in the years since

I'd gotten divorced, he and I had packed up our things and moved to five or six new apartments and several new cities. Still, however, the sight of a box caused him to start trembling.

I picked him up. A building across from our own, the building next door to the funeral parlor, was getting demolished. It had been abandoned for some time, but now, finally, for whatever reason, whoever owned it had decided to tear it down. All day, workers came in and out the front door, carrying armloads of rubble they threw into a dumpster.

Every night, just before sundown, a truck came to remove and empty the dumpster. The driver parked in front of the demolition site, then began to hoist the bed of the truck so the dumpster could be drawn up. Each time, he hoisted the high end of the bed so far that it jammed into the low-hanging branches of an enormous sycamore tree, impacting it so violently that leaves fell in dusty green showers.

At the end of the week, my husband carried our houseplants out to the curb. He placed them under the shade of the sycamore tree, where they sat politely as darkness fell, refusing to protest their unexplained abandonment. That night, the dog wouldn't sleep on the bed. Instead, he huddled under a chair and growled if we tried to pull him out from under his shelter.

THE NEXT MORNING, when we packed the car, all but one of the houseplants was gone. The dog sat on my lap. When we pulled out of our spot, he blinked sorrowfully out the passenger window at the neighborhood we were leaving behind.

It had started to drizzle, and there was an accident on the bridge. By the time we'd reached Manhattan, the rain was coming down in black sheets. It was a Friday afternoon. Approaching the tunnel, the traffic was apocalyptic: it was as though everyone else in the city had also been taken with the urge to flee to far-flung parts of the country.

It took us nearly three hours to get through the tunnel, and by the time we'd reached Pennsylvania, the rain was coming down so hard we had to stop several times and wait by the side of the road. It was night when we started driving in earnest again, heading west toward Harrisburg, and even then, the rain was still falling. By ten o'clock, we were still swimming through a soaking-wet darkness that had been trapped by mountains so gentle and low it seemed to me I could reach out from the window and pat them as I was patting the dog's little skull.

We were only fifty or sixty miles away from New York when we decided it was too late to keep driving. The hotel we found was enormous. It stretched interminably along the side of the highway, but it seemed to be entirely empty except for a handful of construction workers who had, perhaps, been sent to stay there while at work on the highway.

Still, the hotel was operating two separate bars. One was empty, but thumping with music, its darkness ransacked by roving beams of purple light. The other bar was quiet and bright, with a few workers sitting around a long table. My husband ordered a beer. I ordered wine, and the bartender brought me an enormous glass goblet.

On the TV over the bar, newscasters were talking about the rallies in Charlottesville that had happened exactly one year before. There were images of young white men marching toward the capital, carrying tiki torches aloft. All around us, in the quiet bar of that oddly empty hotel, there was the faint murmur of a poorly functioning air conditioner. The wine was so sweet it turned my stomach, so I told my husband I wanted to go back to the room.

He gave me the key, and when I'd climbed the carpeted stairs and walked down the endless hallway, I let myself in and knelt to say hello to the dog. He put his paws on my knees and gazed into my eyes. Later, I took him out for a walk in the field behind the hotel. He sniffed around in the grass, scrupulously gathering evidence. It was after midnight, but purplish light from the city still hung in the sky, so the trees lining the field and the highway stood in silhouette. Standing there while the dog sniffed, I watched them for a while, until suddenly they began to dissolve.

I gaped, in horror, until I realized what was happening: they'd been covered with black birds, which now took flight, abandoning the trees, swarming into the purple light.

When the birds were gone, I realized the trees had lost their leaves. They were obviously dead, though I hadn't seen it. I stared at them for a while, listening to the wash of the cars passing out on the highway. The dog was sitting beside me, shivering in the wet grass. One of his wet paws was on top of my sneaker.

IT TOOK US a week to get from New York to Montana. We stayed one night in Cleveland, empty and shimmering with the heat. There, we took the dog to swim in the lake. We ate barbecue, and it disagreed with my stomach. I spent that night throwing up, crouched on the slate tile of the hotel bathroom.

From Cleveland, we drove to Iowa City, then spent a night in a motel in South Dakota, where we watched a lightning storm cross over the Badlands while a single Chinese teenager cleaned all the rooms. In the morning, he laid out the instant oatmeal packs and the slow cooker full of biscuits and gravy.

When we crossed into Montana, the sky became sooty. On the slopes of the mountains we passed, clumps of trees were burning. Fire trucks were parked at intervals along the road, and, as we drove by, the firemen waved languidly, leaning against the sides of their trucks. For some time, we followed a river so bright it could have been a river of glass. Then we pulled into Bozeman, and onto the street where we'd rented a house.

AS SOON AS we arrived, I got pregnant. Almost immediately, I felt extraordinarily nauseous, a nausea that made the world seem to tilt slightly, as though we were sliding off toward a precipitous edge, so that I often thought of a quote I'd read once and found ridiculous, something Petrarch wrote to a friend, declining a voyage by sea, citing "nausea that would be worse than death." Now I felt I knew what he meant. Sometimes, during those early weeks, I felt so seasick I'd have to claw my way toward the couch to lie down, and then I'd sleep, and when I'd wake hours later, I'd feel so disoriented that I had no idea where I was. Even after I'd recalled the pleather couch in that rented house, and the blue rug, and the empty fireplace that no longer functioned, I still felt I'd woken up on a new planet. The air was different. I couldn't sit up. Certainly, I couldn't write. Everything in my life was suspended, as if to make more room for the nausea.

Meanwhile, everything around us was changing. In New York, the fall had been so hot and muggy the leaves hadn't changed. In Montana, however, the air had grown crisp. There had been a few days of rain, and smoke from the fires had started to clear. Outside our windows, the boughs of the maples that had turned red before the others seemed to be burning, ringed as they were by blazing gold light. One night, the ash tree outside the window was green: the next morning the leaves were all yellow. On windy days, yellow leaves drifted down from the trees, and I moved underneath them: dragging myself to class, disoriented and nauseous.

I DIDN'T TELL anyone I was pregnant. All the websites I was reading warned me to keep it a secret. In the first three months, they cautioned, it's common for something to go wrong. It becomes less common once you know you're pregnant, less common still after six weeks, and less common still after the pregnancy is confirmed by sonogram, but even so: the standard, I learned, was to wait until twelve weeks before telling your secret.

And so, as the weeks passed, six and then eight and then nine, the baby growing from the size of a poppyseed to a cherry, I dragged myself to class, carrying a secret, and missed appointments left and right, and made sure to pretend it was just because I was selfish and careless, and not because of morning sickness.

Finally, on the weekend before the sonogram appointment, which was at ten weeks because the technician had been booked until then, my husband and I went away for a weekend in Glacier National Park. I had decided, for reasons I can no longer remember, that I wanted to write a novel about Mary Shelley and that gloomy summer when she and Percy and Claire were staying in Lord Byron's villa on the glacial shores of Lake Geneva. Sick as I was, however, I was having trouble starting to write. I decided it might be of help to go to Glacier National Park and stand on the shore of a very cold lake.

MARY SHELLEY ARRIVED at that villa, I had learned in my research, after three difficult years. Or maybe it would be better to say that she arrived there after a difficult life. Her mother, Mary Wollstonecraft, the feminist philosopher, had died after giving birth to her. Left to raise a daughter alone, her father, William Godwin, taught Mary to know her mother's radical ideals: that girls should be educated like boys, that women should not be treated like children. That they should know themselves to have values other than beauty, and that marriage, as it then stood, was a monopoly that repressed them. He gave her all her mother's books to read during summers when he sent her to go stay in Scotland. There, alone, she religiously read her mother's books. She absorbed all her mother's ideals, and assumed she shared them with her father, so that later, as a teenager, when she fell in love with

Percy Shelley, she had reason to believe her father would allow her to live with him though he was already married.

Instead, however, her father abruptly disowned her. She was, as a result, parentless and poor when she and Shelley eloped. They took her stepsister, Claire, along with them, and left Shelley's pregnant wife back in London. Together, they traveled to Calais, and from there walked to Paris, passing burnt houses and fields strewn with dead cattle. At night, they didn't rest, but instead wrote in their journals, and when they were finished, they read the complete works of Mary's dead mother.

It was a vivid time in Mary's life. She felt, she said, like a "character in a novel." She felt like a "romance incarnate": as though, once, she had been a mere idea, and now she had been given a body.

When they reached Paris, they walked on to Lucerne. They intended to reach Lake Geneva, but Percy sprained his ankle somewhere near the border. Then they could no longer walk, and their money was running low, so they had to turn back. They traveled along the Rhine, then crossed the channel, disembarking at Gravesend in early September. Virtually penniless—Shelley's rich family had cut him off when he left his pregnant wife—the three of them shared a small lodging in London.

By then, Mary was pregnant. She was often sick, and needed rest, and Percy, who was overjoyed at the birth of his son with the wife he'd abandoned, had, by most accounts, begun an affair with Mary's stepsister, Claire. He liked to take gusty walks out in the country. He liked Mary and Claire to come with him. He was dismayed by Mary's inhibitions when she wouldn't throw off her clothes and jump into a river.

During those months in London, when Mary was pregnant, they were often visited by Shelley's friend Hogg. Shelley, in high spirits, the father of a young son, enjoying his affair with Claire, had begun to profess a hope that Mary would have an affair with Hogg. Though, in principle, as a pure idea, Mary believed in free love, she didn't want to sleep with Hogg. She was very pregnant. He was not—I have checked—an especially attractive man. She tried, however, for Percy's sake, to develop a kind of closeness with Hogg throughout the long months of her pregnancy, and these efforts resulted in a new friendship. In February, she gave birth to her daughter. Two weeks later, the little girl died.

That spring, according to biographers, Mary sank into a deep depression. She was haunted by images of her lost daughter. She wrote to Hogg to tell him that she was no longer a mother. In her journals, she wrote: "Dream that my little baby came to life again—that it had only been cold and that we rubbed it by the fire and it lived—I awake and find no baby—I think about the little thing all day."

That summer, she reconceived. According to her biographers, her depression improved. They say it continued to improve through the waxing months of her new pregnancy. That winter, Claire had an affair with Lord Byron. She ended up pregnant as well. And so perhaps it is true that Mary's situation improved until, in January, she gave birth to a son.

This baby survived. She named him William. He was so small, with a pointy little face, huge, dark eyes, and big ears. She called him Willmouse. That summer, the four of them—

Percy, Claire, Mary, and little Willmouse—traveled toward Lake Geneva to visit Lord Byron again. This time, assisted by a small inheritance Percy had received from an uncle, they didn't run out of money, but crossed through France and Switzerland by rail and coach and finally reached Lake Geneva, where they joined Lord Byron and his doctor, John Polidori. Though it was a "wet, ungenial summer," and Byron was not pleased to learn they'd brought Claire, and John Polidori fell in love with Mary and began to persistently pursue her, so that, still recovering from the birth of her child, she was forced to spend an annoying amount of her time and energy fending off his advances, there were, according to her later accounts, fine moments as well: the hours spent writing, boating on Lake Geneva, talking with friends well into the night.

It was on one of those nights that Byron challenged them all to write a ghost story, and Mary despaired, until finally, after a long conversation about galvanism, electric charge, and the reanimation of corpses (*Dream that my little baby came to life again—that it had only been cold and that we rubbed it by the fire and it lived*), she lay awake during a lightning storm and conceived of the idea that she would expand into her first novel: *Frankenstein*, the story of an ambitious young student who stitches together pieces of corpses, then shocks what was dead back into living.

MY HUSBAND AND I almost didn't go to Glacier National Park. I was getting cramps, and, for a moment, I worried about a miscarriage. But then the cramps stopped, and there was no bleeding, so we set off. But it was a strange trip. I was very nauseous, and it seemed to take ages until we got to the park. That whole drive, we seemed to be tilting off the world's edge into what I could only imagine was an endless nothingness.

For hours, we drove along a long, narrow lake with silvery fingers. Night fell and we were still driving along that long lake. We were somewhere deep in the Crow Reservation. The road was dark, interrupted with less and less frequency by a lamp in the window of an occasional motor home set on the banks of the water. By the time we finally got to the park, the darkness was impossibly thick.

We'd made reservations at the only motel that was still open that late in the season: an old motor inn that faced out onto Lake McDonald. Because we'd arrived after opening hours, we picked up our room key from a box outside the locked office. Then, for a while, hugging our arms in the pitch darkness, we stood there on the stone beach, listening to the sound of the water we couldn't see. Trying to make out the outlines of the mountains that heaved up on the far banks.

Then we went inside to sleep, but I stayed awake. I was thinking about something my husband had said while we were driving along that long lake: an article he'd recently read, about the children of Crow families who were taken away from their parents in order to be given a Christian education. The school must have been drafty and wet, because many of the children died. Their bodies were never returned to their families. They had been buried in mass graves, and who knew, my husband said, how many of their families waited for years for the return of a dead but still beloved small child.

The whole night, I never once fell asleep. Then, when it was finally light, I got out of bed and made myself some oatmeal out of a packet. I put it in a plastic mug, wrapped myself in a wool blanket, and went outside to look at the lake. It was very cold. The lake was the color of pewter, and the hills that rose up around it were covered with the stubs of burnt trees. On the far banks, the mountains were snowy.

WHEN MY HUSBAND finally got up, we went to the office and asked for directions to the Shepard Glacier, the last glacier in North America, but the attendant said the road there was closed for the winter.

We were both disappointed. The glacier, we had been told, was receding every year. Most scientists predicted it would be gone by 2030. And who knew, I thought, standing in that office in October of 2018, twelve years before the demise of the last North American glacier, if we'd ever get back there to see it.

In the end, we went on a different hike. My husband walked slowly, because he knew I felt ill, but while we were hiking, I started feeling more and more nauseous. Then it started snowing. It was strange, feeling so sick, hiking through a burnt forest, while all around us, snow slowly fell. I realized that the fire, whenever it happened, must have burned at almost exactly the height of my head. The trees were only charred to that point, below which their trunks were quilted black satin. Above that line, they weren't burned at all. They were just dead. But the highest boughs were still green, as though they hadn't gotten the message yet.

THE NEXT DAY we drove home. A few minutes into the drive, it started to snow. Then it was snowing too hard to keep driving, so we stopped at a scenic overlook and walked down to a lake. We stood there beside the frozen water in silence. There was a flock of geese at rest on the water. The lake was still as a mirror. But then I raised my arm to point, and suddenly, all at once, the geese lifted into the air, formed a V, and headed south.

After that, we drove for a while longer, until we got to Helena. Helena, the capital of Montana, is a remarkably ugly city. I was so tired I couldn't drive anymore, so we pulled over at Starbucks and I slept for ten minutes in the parking lot. When I woke up, I was freezing. I realized my socks were soaked from that walk down to the lake. I wondered why I was in such a strange mood. Everything, I thought, was exactly as I wanted it to be. I had stepped into the life I wanted to live. Really, I should have been happy.

THE NEXT WEEK, I went to my appointment. In the waiting room, I joined all the other young mothers with various sizes of bellies, and it was so nice: to be in a world inhabited solely by women. I felt immediately welcomed and unusually friendly. When the technician led me into the sonogram room, we chatted about when the baby was due. Then she asked me to lie down. She lathered my belly with cold KY

Jelly, and pressed the knob against my abdomen, and the whole time she was still happily chatting.

She couldn't see a baby up on the screen, so she said maybe she'd have to try it intravaginally. She asked me to put my feet in the stirrups, and even then, both of us were still chatting, but we were also both looking up at the screen, and suddenly the technician stopped talking.

I'd never had a sonogram before, so I didn't know what to look for. What I saw on the screen looked like a cloudy sky, seen from above, with an empty black gap in the upper left corner. I didn't hear any heartbeat. I looked at the technician. Her face had become grim. Her movements with the wand were suddenly more vigorous. They were almost violent. I kept flinching in pain while she made angry measurements.

By the time she'd finished, I'd started crying. She gave me a tissue. Then she gave me another so I could clean off all the lubricant. I asked her what it had meant—the gap, and also the silence—and she said she couldn't interpret the results; it would take a doctor to do that.

Clean off, she told me, and get dressed. And go back to the waiting room until the doctor can see you.

In the waiting room, I felt oddly cold. I zipped up my winter coat. Then I looked around at all the pregnant young women. I realized how foolish I'd been, to imagine that I was one of "the other young mothers." Given my advanced age. And the fact that I was no longer a mother.

· · ·

LATER, WHEN I saw the doctor, she told me the gap in the sky was my empty egg sac. According to her best guess, she said, the baby inside it had most likely developed up to eight weeks, then died, and partially disintegrated. Then it had been reabsorbed back into my body. She sent me home to wait for the miscarriage to happen naturally.

The next day, I had to fly to New York for an event for the book I'd recently published. On the flight, I kept looking out the window at the cloudy gray sky. The little girl who was sitting next to me was watching a movie about a stuffed bear who goes through life as though it's alive: as though it's finally stepped into life, and no longer feels like a character in a novel.

I watched the whole movie over that little girl's shoulder. I couldn't hear the words, so maybe I missed the point, but it seemed to me like an incredibly sad movie: that stuffed bear, surrounded only by humans, with no other bears around to relate to.

Attempting, in an obedient and completely doomed way, to live its fictional bear life as though it had a human body.

WHEN I GOT to New York, I did the event. Then I flew to LA. The miscarriage still hadn't happened naturally, and I was still nauseous. My breasts were still sore. My body seemed simply to have failed to understand it was no longer carrying a baby.

So, finally, I flew back to Montana for the doctor to perform a D&C, a surgical abortion: the removal of what, in my

case, was an embryo that had already died and been mostly—
but not entirely—reabsorbed back into my body.

I WAS AWARE, even then, that some women aren't so lucky.
Some—I had learned, in my last week of googling while
waiting at airports—live in places where it's not possible
to confirm that a miscarriage has been missed by the body.
Others live in places where, because of restrictions on abortion, it's difficult to get a D&C. Such women have to wait
for the miscarriage to happen naturally. In some cases, life-
threatening infections develop. In other cases, nothing happens at all. Instead, the woman is forced to carry her empty
egg sac for years. Over time, the sac hardens, causing lifelong
infertility, or really, lifelong pregnancy, and in some parts of
the world is called a "stone baby."

I considered this on my way back from LA, while I was
waiting for my connection in the Denver airport, somewhat
numb, wandering the terminals in something of a stupor, a
stone woman waiting to go home to have them remove my
stone baby.

For a while, I looked for a Starbucks I never found. Then
I stopped at a newsstand and picked up a magazine and read
an article about Kavanaugh's confirmation—Trump calling
him "this innocent man; this good and decent man"—and
looked at a picture of him with his wife and two daughters,
and also a picture of the woman who had come forward
and faced vicious harassment—death threats to herself and
her family, public speculation about her involvement in the
drug trade and international orgies—in order to put on the

record the fact that, when she was a teenager, he'd tried to rape her.

He continued to try to undress her though she asked him to stop, and even tried to push him away. But still, he continued to try, and she couldn't stop him, because he was strong and drunk and persistent. She was entirely out of control of the situation, in other words, a very scared little girl, and he was only eventually stopped by his drunken confusion about the one-piece bathing suit she was wearing under her shorts.

I turned the page. Then I read an article about how many of the immigrant families that had been divided at the border still hadn't been reunited: because no one at ICE kept clear records about who they'd split from whom in the first place; because many of their parents had been induced to self-deport in order to preserve the possibility of reuniting one day with their babies.

Then, without paying, I put the magazine back and walked through the terminal to my gate. I thought about how many babies were currently living in camps. How many toddlers, abruptly weaned, were no longer speaking. How many were now wetting the bed. Were there night-lights, I wondered, at the camps? For babies who were afraid of the darkness?

Then, trying to turn my mind to something else, I thought about that stuffed bear in the movie. Who—if I'd understood it correctly—somehow showed up at the train station, parentless and alone, carrying the contact information for a family he'd never met. At which point he had to find his own way through the city, even though everyone was pushing him on the escalator, shoving past him, because he wasn't as tall as an actual person.

EVEN AFTER THE operation was finished, I still didn't feel any different. I was still cripplingly nauseous all day. Fall was over. Now it was winter, and when I went outside, my nipples ached in the cold.

When, walking to work, or heading downtown to pick up a coffee, I remembered the surgery, it seemed to me that it was nothing more than a series of different waiting rooms. In the first one, my husband and I sat side by side, reading a religious magazine that had been placed there, presumably, because it was a Christian hospital. This magazine claimed evidence had been found proving that dinosaurs lived at the same time as humans.

Then a nurse came and led us into the next waiting room. I lay down on a hospital bed in my clothes, and while another nurse was preparing my shots, she asked if this was our first baby. I said yes, and she said, Ah, I'm so sorry. I'll pray for you and your family.

Then another nurse came, and wheeled me along a hospital corridor. My husband walked alongside us. In the next waiting room, I changed into a blue gown. Below the blue hem, my legs and bare feet emerged, thin and strikingly pale, the legs and feet of an innocent virgin. I looked up at a crucifix on the wall while leaning over the bed with my gown pulled up so the nurse could give me more shots.

Then the anesthesiologist came in to introduce himself. He asked me if we'd been trying to have a baby. I told him we had. Ah, he said, and patted my hand. Once he had departed, a new nurse arrived to wheel me into the last waiting room, a place where my husband could no longer follow. And finally, from there, they wheeled me toward the operating room. Then, though it seemed as though I'd been waiting forever, things suddenly began to move very fast. There was a rush to open the doors, and then we were in a cold room, so cold that one of the last things I saw was a plume of my own breath. I also saw that the room was bare, full of clean metal, a room like a capsule sent into space, but I didn't have much time to observe anything else, because they were shifting me onto a large metal table, and one nurse was holding my hand while another nurse put a mask over my face, and I didn't have time to think anymore because the room was fading away, and I may have imagined this, but it seemed to me that somewhere, in the background, somebody was praying.

LATER, WHEN I came to, I realized it was all over. I cried for a few minutes. Then that, too, was behind me. It was very quiet. I was alone. They'd drawn a blue curtain around me. After a while, a nurse came with ice chips in a wax paper cup, which I scooped out with my paws, and chewed, listening to the sound of my teeth crunching, until they wheeled me out to the second recovery room where I was able to sit with my husband.

To kill time, I asked him what he'd done while I was in the surgery. He said he'd gone to the cafeteria. I asked him what he ate. He told me he ate half of a turkey wrap, a V8, a bag of baby carrots, and a large slice of chocolate cake. Then we sat together in silence, until finally I thought that I should call my mother. She asked if I was alone. I told her that, no, my husband was with me. She told me I was lucky. When she herself had undergone this surgery, her husband, my father, hadn't been allowed to come with her. She'd been alone, she told me, when she was recovering.

Then the nurse came in, so I hung up with my mother, and listened while she gave me my postsurgery instructions. Finally, with her permission, I changed out of my hospital gown and put on my own clothes again. Then we left the hospital. It was a bright, wintry day when we walked out through the sliding glass doors and I stepped back into life, dressed as my former self, though now newly empty.

It was dizzying, to be back in the same world in such a different state: full when I went in, now totally empty.

IN THE WAKE of that surgery, everyone—the doctor I saw, my friends, my mother—told me how common it was. Miscarriage, they told me, is another one of these things, like eating disorders and rape, that happen to most women.

In the weeks and months that followed the surgery, I found this refrain a little enraging. Why, I wondered, should I have to take comfort in the commonness of female suffering? At the same time, however, I knew it was true. And that, in fact, on the spectrum of miscarriage trauma, mine fell very low.

I had a friend, for instance, who had learned of her missed miscarriage at twelve weeks, rather than ten, and after she'd already seen her baby's heartbeat. I counted two friends who had three miscarriages each. One of those friends had a sister who had five miscarriages before giving up on having a baby.

I thought of my friend whose water broke when she was four months pregnant, and who went into labor, and who believed for some hours that they might be able to save the baby, only to learn that the baby had died, at which point she lost consciousness for a while, or couldn't remember what happened next, and only came to when a nun arrived to let her know they'd made a coffin for her lost child.

My mother went into labor when she was five months pregnant. She'd been trying to get pregnant for years. For five months, she carried a child. Then she went into labor and lost the baby.

Once, in Texas, I worked for a woman who learned when she was four months pregnant that her baby would only live a few days after his birth. And so—because new laws had been passed in Texas, and by then it was too late for her to abort the pregnancy—she carried the baby to term. And labored for nearly three days. And finally gave birth to a boy with wide-set eyes and webbed toes, who wailed, and climbed onto her chest, and comforted himself by giving suck, and lived in her arms until the next morning.

These were women I thought about in the days that followed my D&C, when I'd started bleeding, and the cramping began. I thought about them, and I also thought about Mary Shelley, whose baby lived for three weeks. How hard, I thought, when the cramping had stopped, and the bleeding had slowed, and the nausea had finally faded away. How hard, I thought, somewhat numbly, moving through my life unfeeling, as though I were living in a waking dream. How hard to have held it. How hard to have known it.

It was so cold during those winter months. All through them, I felt as though I was floating in the coldness of space, looking back on my life from a great distance.

THAT WINTER, I was still trying to write my novel about Mary Shelley. But I kept sending myself down endless research rabbit holes. First about galvanism, and the discovery of electricity, which occurred in Shelley's lifetime and inspired the methods she gave Frankenstein. Then I read about Arctic exploration, the frame in which Shelley chose to set Frankenstein's story.

For weeks, in that cold house, I read about Arctic exploration in the nineteenth century. Then I began reading about its contemporary equivalent: the exploration of space. Astronauts, I learned at some point during that winter, when I spent a lot of time listlessly searching Wikipedia, are changed by their travels through the universe. They age differently from people who stay on Earth. Their telomeres—the caps that prevent strands of DNA from decay, and shorten throughout the course of a lifetime—lengthen in space, as though they were growing younger. Later, however, when the astronauts return to Earth, the shortening of their telomeres accelerates unnaturally, overtaking the telomeres of those who never embarked on a space journey, so that they who were once younger become older than they were when they embarked on the journey.

Similarly, though the astronauts' rates of cognition remain stable and even improve when they're in space, they slow upon their return, so that they who were once smarter now become a little less clever. Which is all only to say that the men who landed on the moon were changed by the experience. One, Edgar Mitchell, left NASA upon his return to start a foundation dedicated to the study of human consciousness. Another, James Irwin, had an epiphany while on the moon and, immediately upon his return, resigned from the air force to found an evangelical church. A third, Alan Bean, returned to Earth after landing on the moon and became a full-time painter.

He painted nothing but the moon. Once, describing his decision to become a painter, Bean told someone that he had been fortunate enough to travel to a place no artist's eye had ever been. As such, he felt compelled to translate the experience. But the task wasn't easy. He had to figure out, he said, how to add color. In some of his paintings of the moon, he used real moondust. He was able to do this when he realized that some of the keepsake patches from his moon suit were dirty. He also incorporated into his artistic process the hammer that had been used to pound the flagpole into the lunar surface, as well as a moon boot. It was hard, but he felt consumed by the importance of the task. He felt himself, he said, years later, still painting the moon, to be the only one who could possibly do it.

Describing his own radical change, James Irwin once said: "We lived on another world that was completely 'ours' for three days. It must have been very much like the feelings of Adam and Eve when the Earth was 'theirs.' How to describe it, how to describe it."

I read that quote from Irwin (*how to describe it, how to describe it*) a few weeks after I had been released from the hospital. That night, I couldn't sleep, so I went downstairs for a glass of milk. I stood by the kitchen window, looking up at the moon. It was easy for me, that night, to imagine that, if you had gone to the moon, it would be difficult upon your return.

For some time after, I thought, you would feel lost and lonely. You would wander around, thinking no one could understand what you'd seen. You would try to find a way to describe it. You'd be the only person who'd know if your description was right.

Perhaps, I thought, it is helpful, in such a state, to start a foundation, or an evangelical church. Or to become a painter who paints nothing but the moon you were fortunate enough to once visit.

FOR WEEKS AFTER the surgery, I still had pregnancy dreams, those oddly vivid dreams that some people hypothesize are a result of pregnancy hormones, and others theorize are simply the result of intense feeling during the day: the strangely alert state of waiting that comes along with pregnancy.

One night, for instance, a week or so after the surgery, I dreamed I'd had a baby as small as a religious figurine. It was a pale ivory deity the size of a cherry. It had an elephant's snout. Lying in my hospital bed, I held it carefully in the palm of my hand.

My room was fluorescently lit, but it was dark outside the hospital window, and I could see light glistening over the water that had surged up around it. I was completely alone.

I realized there must have been a hurricane in the night, and that everyone in the hospital had already fled. Finally comprehending my state, I got up, carefully, and began to wander around the hospital. I was wearing my blue gauze gown. My feet were bare, and I was walking like a lost little girl, looking around for someone to help me. But the building was completely abandoned. Finally, still carrying my baby, I wandered down to the lobby, where I discovered—lucky for me—that the dog was waiting in a rowboat tethered to the main entrance doors.

He was shivering, wet and cold, but still loyally waiting. I tucked the baby carefully into the pocket of my gauze gown, then waded out to the boat. In it, the dog and the baby and I set out into the darkness. I was rowing us through the streets of our old Brooklyn neighborhood, though now, of course, they were more like canals, and the oars slipped through black rustling waters.

The first stories of brownstones were completely submerged, so we rowed past second-floor windows. And when we came to my husband's old building, the one where he was living back when we first met, we moored the rowboat in a tree and climbed in through a fire escape.

Then, for a while, with water up to our knees, the dog and the baby and I wandered around the old, empty building. Then the dog asked why I couldn't find my husband's apartment. I closed my eyes, and—as if in my own defense—said, "I'm just trying to remember his face."

And then I woke, and lay beside my husband and looked at his face, asleep on a pillow under a window that had been fanged with icicles. It was different from the face I'd remembered. Quietly, I got up and slipped out of the bedroom before the dog could come with me. Then I went to my desk and thought about Mary Shelley.

THOSE YEARS—BOTH before and after Mary Shelley conceived of *Frankenstein*, when she gave birth to the daughter who died, then to the son who lived, and shortly after was pregnant again—must have been full of strange dreams, like the "waking dream" she described in the introduction she later wrote for *Frankenstein*: a "pale student of unhallowed arts kneeling beside the thing he had put together," watching when the creature started to stir, noting its "uneasy, half-vital motion."

"Frightful," she wrote in that introduction, describing her pale student's reaction. "Frightful it must be; for supremely frightful would be the effect of any human endeavor to mock the stupendous mechanism of the Creator."

IT WAS INTERESTING, in the weeks after that surgery, to reread that introduction: an account written by a woman, and a writer, who had given birth to two babies in two years, describing how frightful it must be to give life to a creature.

"His success," Shelley wrote, "would terrify the artist;"

he would rush away from his odious handywork,
horror-stricken. He would hope that, left to itself,
the slight spark of life which he had communicated
would fade; that this thing, which had received such

imperfect animation, would subside into dead matter; and he might sleep in the belief that the silence of the grave would quench forever the transient existence of the hideous corpse which he had looked upon as the cradle of life. He sleeps; but he is awakened; he opens his eyes; behold the horrid thing stands at his bedside, opening his curtains, and looking on him with yellow, watery, but speculative eyes.

I opened mine in terror. The idea so possessed my mind, that a thrill of fear ran through me, and I wished to exchange the ghastly image of my fancy for the realities around. I see them still; the very room, the dark parquet, the closed shutters, with the moonlight struggling through, and the sense I had that the glassy lake and white high Alps were beyond. I could not so easily get rid of my hideous phantom; still it haunted me. I must try to think of something else. I recurred to my ghost story,—my tiresome unlucky ghost story! O! if I could only contrive one which would frighten my reader as I myself had been frightened that night!

So I read, in the weeks after my surgery, when I myself had also conceived a creature of imperfect animation, a creature who—I had been told, and yet I could not quite believe, since after all the symptoms of pregnancy had continued—had subsided again into dead matter. It was interesting. It was very interesting, the way the student wakes and goes to his creation, goes to what he had once imagined was the cradle of life, and finds, instead, a transient existence: a creature not dead and not fully living.

And so, too, in the next paragraph, Mary Shelley emerges from her waking dream and finds that, in conjuring these characters, she has created something frightening, something *off*, something one half step away from really living, and yet somehow all the more affecting. She wishes she could un-create her creature, but finds that, though it isn't quite human, and it isn't quite living, its partial existence has changed everything about reality: the dark parquet, the closed shutters, the glassy lake, the Alps, and the struggling moonlight.

IN MONTANA, IN the weeks after that surgery, we received a bill for eight thousand dollars, because while "medical" as opposed to "optional" D&Cs were covered by our insurance, our insurance had an eight-thousand-dollar deductible. Then, too, I continued to have vivid and terrible dreams.

Also, it got very cold. Everyone said it was the coldest winter they could remember: a truly world-ending, apocalyptic winter. To make things worse, the heat in the house we were renting kept breaking.

We had started trying to have a baby again. Each month, I waited. It was different, now, than it had been before. Something had shifted in me, and suddenly I didn't only vaguely think I might want one, I was sure I wanted six or seven babies. Then a pipe froze, and burst, and the water that leaked into the bathtub froze, and for several days there was a layer of ice in the tub that I could have skimmed off the surface and held up to my face.

One night in December, after such a cold day, I had a

long, elaborate dream that I had been placed in a storage unit for women who couldn't get pregnant. It was a refrigerated room, like the meat lockers at the back of grocery stores. They kept it clean and bare. At the center of the unit, there was a long, rectangular, metal table. There were middle school lockers lining the walls. The room was very cold, much colder than the frozen-food aisle, so all the women who stayed in the unit wore their puffy coats all the time. At night, we hung them on hooks, and climbed into our individual lockers to sleep. In the mornings, we emerged and gathered around the long table to work at the dismal jobs we'd been given.

This shared communal schedule, however, did not produce feelings of female solidarity. In the dream, sitting uselessly at my place at the table, I felt nothing but loathing for all those other women. There they were, working at their dumb jobs, as though they still believed they made a difference. Sitting there at the metal table, looking at those other infertile women, it seemed to me that their faces had been cut out of magazines and pasted on the bodies of stuffed bears. They lumbered around the storage unit with their sad, cotton-stuffed bodies.

Obediently, when the time came to report to the vitamin dispensary, they took prenatal vitamins. Then they reported back to the table, where they pretended to work, blinking their black glass eyes at their laptops, typing badly with their clumsy plush paws.

It must have been obvious that I hated everyone else, because the other women avoided me also. They did, however, talk with one another: in line at the watercooler, or the vitamin dispensary, holding wax paper cups in their paws.

Because the only thing they had in common was the fact that all of them had miscarried or couldn't get pregnant, they spent all their time talking about how long they'd held on to their babies.

Everyone was busy making calculations of weeks. A hierarchy developed, based on the length of time women had maintained their pregnancies, and therefore the size of their sorrows. One woman carried hers for twenty weeks. Another held on for eight months. Theirs were the predominate sorrows in our particular unit.

Sometimes, one or two of the women stopped working and trundled over to the swinging doors, where they stuck their snouts into the crack. As it turned out, the room was, in fact, at the back of a grocery store, and, through the crack, you could see actual women, shopping in the actual store. For the sake of those women, pushing their carts full of food and smiling babies, we women in the unit didn't ever push our way through the blue doors. We all knew how upsetting our presence could be for the unstuffed, actual women with families.

I say "we," but, in the dream, it was a point of pride in my life that I never went to look through the door. Proudly, I made a practice of setting myself apart from the women. Instead, I waited stubbornly at my place at the table, making macaroni necklaces on a round paper plate.

Occasionally, my husband came to the unit to visit. Then, when the unit lights had been turned out for the night, he lay down with me in my locker. He held my stuffed-bear body in his living arms. "I love you," he said, and I lay beside him in silence, thinking about those other women trundling around with their bear snouts.

"You can come home," he said. "We don't have to do this."

But I stayed where I was. And later, first thing in the morning, I watched him leave through the blue doors because he had real work to do: Real ice to clear from the bathtub. Real snow to shovel in the real driveway. And me, returning to the work of arranging my macaroni.

DURING THE DAY, I tried to return to my writing. But it had become difficult for me to write. Every time I sat down to work, I thought how much less I cared about writing a novel than having a baby.

Sometimes, in the months after my release from the hospital, I wondered about the relationship between writing and having babies. When I was in graduate school, I had often been shocked to encounter the reviews—written by men—of the earliest women poets writing in English: how often those reviewers implied—or said outright—that these women's energies would have been better spent rearing children.

Was it an either/or? I used to think. Was one related in any way to the other? It seemed to be an impossibly antiquated idea. And yet. Once, in a twenty-first-century reading I later did in Los Angeles to promote my second novel, a woman asked why I had made the decision to write instead of having a baby. At a reading I did in Massachusetts for the same book, a book about artificial intelligence, a man told me he found that women's writing was better when it was about personal subjects: marriage, for instance, or having babies. At a reading I did in Paris, a man raised his hand to ask a question, then went on at great length about how women were well prepared to write stories because of the experience of carrying a baby: that hollowness, that emptiness, that can only be filled by conceiving a character.

At the time, mentally, I heaped scorn upon him: Must the experience of womanhood, I thought, entail carrying a baby? But in fact, in those weeks after my release from the hospital, I began to feel that perhaps he was correct. There was, I began to suspect, a hollowness, an emptiness, that I now carried within me: one that, perhaps, could only be filled by a creature. Up to that point in my life, it had been enough—more than enough—to fill whatever emptiness was within me by conceiving characters. But something had changed. It was almost as though, now that I had come so close to conceiving an actual creature—not some flimsy character, not a half person on a page—I could no longer feel that my writing had any value, not to myself, or to anyone else whomsoever.

SOME WEEKS LATER in that absurdly cold winter, a winter when I found it hard to write because now it was impossible for me not to compare writing to having a baby, and to find writing to be a profession less vital, less meaningful, than having a baby (though of course the two are quite different pursuits, and a man would never think, Perhaps this is writing I'll do instead of having a baby, or Is this a substitute for having a baby?, or This is something I'll do to make my body less empty), I went back to the hospital.

I didn't need to go back. They'd told me I didn't need to return until I was pregnant again, and I wasn't pregnant. Still, we had been trying for several months, and I woke up that morning and felt sure that they should run blood tests.

I called the nurse twice, but no one called back, and because it was a Friday, and one's life, when one is trying to get pregnant, becomes darkly marked by each passing week, I convinced myself that the question was urgent. Then I decided that, since I wasn't doing anything else, perhaps I should simply stop by the office.

As soon as I'd parked in the same lot where I used to park when I was pregnant, and walked in again through entrance 3B, I realized I'd made an awful mistake. No one wanted me in that office. I'd come, uninvited, dragging my embarrassing grieving.

There I was, walking down the same hallway, past that long panorama of snowy mountains under a sunset, and I felt like I had a bomb in my pocket. I knew for sure that I should turn back. But still, having started down that terrible path, I felt determined to finish, so I headed into the office, and waited in line to see the receptionist, and when my turn came up, I sat down in front of her. I explained that I didn't have an appointment.

Her smile faded. In that soothing, professional voice that flight attendants use when they're trying to keep an unhinged person from disturbing the other passengers, she told me the nurse would call as soon as she found herself free.

All around the waiting room, noting the potential disturbance, the round, pregnant young women eyed one another nervously. They put careful, maternal hands on their bellies.

They were all part of the same tribe, citizens of the same lucky country, aligned for their own safety against me.

ON THE WAY home, I passed cross-country skiers practicing on the course behind the hospital. Then I turned into town, and found they were holding some sort of rally, so that the streets were no longer sleepy and charming, but instead scary with revving engines and sudden explosions.

For a moment, I saw what was really around me: the trucks with Trump bumper stickers, Confederate flags, white supremacist decals; the motorcycles with their exhaust pipes altered to spew out plumes of black smoke; the T-shirts with images of handguns and assault weapons.

And then I kept driving, and stopped paying attention to the motorcycles and the trucks, and when I got home, my husband was eating soup and listening to sports radio.

I didn't tell him about going to the hospital. Instead, I told him about the white supremacist decals and the modified engines. He listened and nodded. What else could he do? Then he went out to shovel snow, and I went up to the room where it no longer made sense to me to do any writing: not about the scene outside our house, not about the hospital, not even about Mary Shelley, though I'd gone to the Country Bookshelf and purchased several large books, including one enormous biography of Percy Shelley, which the woman at the counter had given to me with a sigh, as though she were tired of selling people such heavy books about men like Percy Shelley. There it was on my shelf, taking up so much room, but I didn't want to open it. Nor did

I want to write about Mary Shelley. Nor did I want to write about anything else on the planet.

No. I tried, sitting there at my computer, but really just nothing came into my mind, and so I sat there with the dog at my feet, looking through the icicled window, and thought about how happy I had been only one year ago, before we moved, before I was pregnant, before I ever thought about Mary Shelley.

Had I really rested in those patches of sunlight? Had I really read about Moomins, had I really been happy? Or was I just happy in the way people get angry so they don't have to feel guilty, or anxious so they don't have to feel depressed? Or vicious so they don't have to feel helpless? Or happy, so very happy they don't have to feel anything other than overwhelming happiness.


ALL THAT WINTER, it was difficult for me to write. And yet. One has to go on. And so I forged ahead with my novel about Mary Shelley. In the following weeks, for instance, I learned that, in the years that followed the summer when she first conceived of *Frankenstein*, Shelley always made a point of how happy she was during those dark and gloomy months, when the weather was strange and a pandemic raged and she and Percy and Claire were staying in a villa with Lord Byron and John Polidori.

In her 1831 introduction, she wrote:

And now, once again, I bid my hideous progeny go forth and prosper. I have an affection for it, for it was the offspring of happy days, when death and grief were but words, which found no true echo in my heart. Its several pages speak of many a walk, many a drive, and many a conversation, when I was not alone; and my companion was one who, in this world, I shall never see more.

Happy days, then, the dark days of that summer, when Mary Shelley conceived of a creature.

READING SUCH LINES, during that long winter after miscarrying a pregnancy, it was hard for me to feel that she was being perfectly truthful. Was she, I asked myself, really so happy? With that husband? And just over a year after the death of her baby?

But perhaps, I said to myself, part of why those years later seemed so happy to Mary Shelley was the incredible cascade of personal tragedies that followed the summer of her first literary progeny. That fall, the fall of 1816, she and Shelley and their baby boy—their little Willmouse—returned to England, where they took lodgings in Bath, near separate lodgings they'd found for Claire. There, they lived together frugally, while Mary struggled to finish her travelogues and *Frankenstein.* She wanted to publish them to make an income, since Shelley was still cut off from his family, and he wasn't making money with his poetry.

She worked until October, when her half sister, Fanny, killed herself with laudanum. Then, in December, Harriet, the wife Shelley abandoned, drowned herself in a lake.

At the end of that month, Mary and Percy decided to get married, not because he wanted to, but at the advice of his lawyers, who believed it would help him regain custody of his two children with his former wife. But in March, the courts ruled against Shelley, and his children were placed with a local family. Then Claire, along with her daughter, moved in with the Shelleys. The five of them moved to a large, damp building on the banks of the Thames.

By then, Mary was pregnant for a third time. She was tired and often sick, but nevertheless, she forced herself to finish her books. In September, she gave birth to a daughter. Later the same month, her travelogues were published, to some acclaim. Their publication, however, did little to alleviate the financial concerns she and Shelley faced, and it was at that point that Shelley began to live away from the damp house on the Thames in order to evade his creditors.

That winter, raising two children alone, Mary published *Frankenstein*. Most critics believed it had been written by Percy. Those who accepted that it was written by Mary felt that her gender was the source of its flaws. It was largely panned; occasionally, critics praised the influence of Percy's poetry.

Then Percy began to show symptoms of ill health, aggravated by an unusually dark and cold winter, and so for the sake of his lungs, and to avoid his creditors, Mary and Shelley and Claire decided to leave England forever. They intended to rove: to read and write and wander freely. To that end, their first stop was in Venice, where they left Claire's baby with Byron, who had agreed to raise her as long as Claire had no more interactions with him. They stayed in Venice through September. It was there that Mary's new baby, Clara, died of a fever.

From Venice, they moved to Naples. There, Mary was often ill, and suffered from the loss of her daughter, and Percy wrote poems regretting his wife's preoccupation ("my dearest Mary, wherefore hast thou gone, and left me in this dreary world alone") and registered the birth and death of a baby girl out of wedlock.

From Naples, a city Mary later called a paradise inhabited by devils, they moved on to Rome, where Mary became pregnant again and began work on a new novel, which she abandoned in June, when Willmouse also died of a fever. He'd been alive for a little over three years. In a letter to a friend, she wrote: "May you my dear Marianne never know what it is to lose two only and lovely children in one year—to watch their dying moments—and then at last to be left childless."

No longer a mother, she turned back to her writing. Over the next several months, she wrote and nearly finished the novel *Matilda*. In November, she gave birth to a son, then went back to writing *Matilda*: a novel written furiously about the abuse of a young girl by her father. By the summer of 1822, she was pregnant again. Then, from Rome, she and Percy and Claire moved in with friends—Jane and Edward Williams—who had rented a villa at the sea's edge on the Bay of Lerici. The villa was isolated, dark, and remote, and Mary came to refer to it as a dungeon. It was there that Percy broke the news that Claire's daughter with Lord Byron had died of typhus in the convent school where Byron had sent her.

It was there, also, that Mary miscarried, and lost so much

blood that she nearly died. Afterward, she fell into another depression. Percy spent more time that summer with Jane Williams than he did with her. All the poems he wrote during those months are addressed not to Mary, not even to Claire, but instead to Jane Williams.

In July, he and Edward went out in a boat to sail down the coast to Livorno. They never returned. Ten days later, when his body was found washed ashore, his wife and his friends cremated it on the beach at Viareggio. From there, Mary returned to London, where she devoted herself to taking care of her son and to finishing *The Last Man*, her final novel and second work of science fiction, a book about England sometime in the twenty-first century, ravaged by an unknown, deadly pandemic, and the loneliness of the last man as he wanders through it.

BY FEBRUARY, I was pregnant again. I was still pregnant in March. It remained unusually cold in Montana. And, as with the last time I'd been pregnant, I was exceedingly nauseous: not just in the morning but all day and all night, so that sometimes I woke up and couldn't fall back asleep because I was so nauseous.

It was, for me, an extraordinarily isolating state: that nausea, which consumed every hour of the day, and which no one could have understood even if I'd been able to tell them about it. Then, too, even after I'd gotten through the eight-week appointment, I still worried all the time. Since the last time I hadn't known when the pregnancy ended, or when my body began reabsorbing the baby, and since I had believed the whole time that everything was going fine, I didn't trust myself to know when something awful had happened.

In April, at the last minute, I decided I couldn't take another cold, nauseous, uncertain week, so my husband and I made plans to go to Las Vegas, the one warm place we could reach with a direct flight. I thought a trip might make me feel better, but Las Vegas is a strange place. Flying toward it, you see that it rises abruptly and completely artificially out of the desert, as if it were the elaborate set for an expensive science fiction film, or a domed city on some other planet.

Our affordable and otherwise basically unremarkable Airbnb included a limo ride from the airport. We were picked up from a parking garage that was connected to the terminal, so we never went outside into the desert heat. Instead, we transitioned from the Montana cold to the air-conditioning of the flight to the refrigerated back seat, which was enormous, so that we ended up sitting quite far away from each other.

In some ways, I realized, we hadn't quite gotten our closeness back since I was first pregnant, and extraordinarily nauseous, then no longer pregnant, and absorbed in the strange dreams that seemed to expand to take up the space of my new and awful emptiness, so we sat two cold miles apart. We didn't talk. I faced the window and watched while the exits on the mass of intertwined highways lifted their heads and flicked their tongues around us.

For a while, it was just highway. But then we started to see the casinos, and the glinting gold façade of the Mandalay Bay Hotel. It was, I suddenly remembered, the hotel where the shooter was staying who killed all those people at the country music festival, back when my husband and I were still in New York, when my parents' street still hadn't been swept away, when the leaves still hadn't fallen off the ginkgo trees and I was still so terrifically happy.

While we drove past, I craned my neck. For some reason, I expected his window to be marked—blacked out, perhaps, or covered in yellow police tape—but it wasn't: all the gleaming black windows were identical to one another, as though none of them had ever been broken to allow an assault weapon to slide out.

OUR APARTMENT WAS at the Palms. There was a free minibar, an abundance of shiny pillows on the bed, and a small balcony overlooking the highway. In the gleaming chrome-and-faux-marble bathroom there were matching white bathrobes draped over hangers on hooks facing the mirror: twin ghosts lurking behind us.

Once we'd settled in, we took the skywalk to the casino. I wanted to have a drink at the bar with the shark tank by Damien Hirst: *The Physical Impossibility of Death in the Mind of Someone Living.* I had a seltzer with lime, and my husband had a beer, and we sat there looking up at the belly of a dead shark while the bartender told us that at one point the shark had begun to decay. Somehow the formaldehyde in the tank had gone bad, so they had to drain it and repair the dead shark and suspend it again in new liquid.

Later, my husband went to play slots and I had another seltzer with lime and the same bartender told me that the casino had just finished construction of its most expensive suite, a two-story sky villa with six stand-alone pieces by Damien Hirst. It was called the "Empathy Suite." It had a cantilevered pool and a gym, and the artworks included a diamond-filled pill cabinet, flooring inlaid with dead butterflies, and a tank with not one but two suspended tiger sharks. You could rent it for two hundred thousand dollars a night.

For a moment, I considered flirting with the bartender, just to see if I still knew how. But then I felt too nauseous to flirt, or even to stay at the bar, so I went back to the room. I tried to fall asleep, but I couldn't, nauseous as I was, drowning in that sea of decorative pillows. So then I put on my bathrobe and went out to the balcony. The cars passing below on the highway sounded like a conch shell held up to my ear. If I closed my eyes, I could almost imagine I was on a balcony overlooking the ocean, which led me to look up tiger sharks on my phone, and to learn that they were endangered as a result of overfishing.

Then I thought about Trump announcing his intention to gut the Endangered Species Act, and I thought again about that tank over the bar: *The Physical Impossibility of Death in the Mind of Someone Living.* Then I looked up the Las Vegas massacre, and read that by the time police had broken into the shooter's room at the Mandalay Bay Hotel, he'd already killed 58 people and wounded 422 others, and that another 429 were wounded in the ensuing stampede.

I turned off my phone. Then I went inside and got a bag of pretzels from the free minibar, then went outside again and listened to the sound of the ocean, and then my husband came back from the casino. He reported that he'd lost seven dollars and watched several men get approached by prostitutes. Then he got a bag of Cheetos from the minibar, changed into his bathrobe, and sat with me for a while on the balcony.

Ghost versions of ourselves, we looked out over the city. Because it was so bright, even at night, we could see the mountains in the distance. He told me he'd heard once that those mountains were composed entirely of the skeletons of sea creatures. Once, they were alive in the ocean that used to stretch over Las Vegas. Then they'd died, and their bodies settled down into heaps of other bodies, bodies reabsorbed into bodies that later solidified and became mountains on the floor of the ocean. And then the oceans had dried up, and now they were a jagged black line, drawn against the gray sky beyond them.

IN THE MORNING, we tried to go down to the casino to have breakfast, but an alarm began to go off. Strangely, however, no one in the casino seemed worried at all. At the craps tables, people kept playing craps. In the casino café, people were calmly eating glazed pastries. And meanwhile, in the background, the alarm bell was screaming.

My husband and I went outside to the parking lot. We sat on a bench next to a palm tree in a gold pot, and he told me again about the time he was in a stampede in Penn Station. It was rush hour, the spring after Trump was elected, and a policeman shot a homeless man with a taser. Then people assumed there was an active shooter somewhere in the station, so a stampede started in the Amtrak pavilion.

My husband had been waiting to come visit me at a

residency in upstate New York. While I was away, he was looking after the dog, so he was standing near the departures board with the dog between his feet, and, in the stampede, the dog slipped away. My husband ended up in Hudson Booksellers, hiding with a bunch of terrified strangers.

All around him, people were curled in the fetal position and praying, and most people had covered their heads, but my husband told me he stayed on his knees. For some reason, he said, he wanted to be able see if the shooter approached him.

Later, when people realized there wasn't any real danger, they began to get up off the ground and head out of the station. But my husband had to stay and search for the dog. So there he was, wandering around the empty station, which was now littered with plastic bottles and single shoes, abandoned handbags, suitcases with their guts spilled out over the floor, but no little dog dragging his leash, until finally a woman who had been sitting on the floor before the stampede, and remained sitting there once it was over, called to him and told him his dog had passed by. Reassured, though he had no idea how she'd known that it was a dog he was searching for, my husband kept looking, until finally a voice came over the loudspeaker: a security guard had a little dog. My husband picked him up and took the subway to Brooklyn.

IT WAS A long time before the alarm stopped going off. When it finally did, I was too nauseous to eat, so I went back to the room. I sat on the balcony and read a book about the storage of nuclear waste in Las Vegas, and the various failed proposals that politicians came up with to invent a language that could warn future civilizations about the presence of nuclear danger, until my husband came back with ginger ale and a bunch of bananas, which I ate, slowly, overlooking the highway.

By then it was nearly noon and we decided to go to the pool, but there was something wrong with the elevator. We waited for almost half an hour before it finally came, and when it did come it was packed. Still, we squeezed ourselves in, but then it stopped at every floor on the way down to the pool.

By the seventeenth floor, it was so full that my husband and I were pressed into the back corner. We were next to a disabled man in his wheelchair. He was facing the back mirror. Next to him, there was a cheerful, leathery man with a margarita in a plastic cup.

This man, by making loud jokes about who we should permit into the elevator and who we should reject, had made himself a sort of leader. Sometimes, when the door opened, our merry leader said, "It's too full, you can't get on." And sometimes, particularly if it was a pair of women he considered pretty, he'd give his allies a sly smile and say, "We can make room for two little ladies." And every time we shifted around to let a new person on, we jostled the disabled man's wheelchair.

For his part, he remained calm. Maybe he was used to getting wedged into small spaces. But I was thinking about the baby inside me, how its brain and its heart were still forming, how it was an extraordinarily tiny and vulnerable creature, and how this was the world I was bringing it into, and by the time we got out of the elevator, I had to sit down on a bench in the lobby. Then I started crying, and I couldn't stop. There I was, in the lobby of the hotel, surrounded by people, crying so hard that my husband eventually gave me his baseball hat to pull down over my face.

By the next day, we were back in Montana, and though it was still very cold, and the park was still covered in snow, I found I didn't mind so much. It was nice to walk out of the door in the morning and smell pine needles and ice on the cement, and so the days passed until the twelve-week appointment, when they did another ultrasound and told me the baby was healthy.

MEANWHILE, I WAS still trying to write a novel about Mary Shelley: a novel about how, for instance, when she was a girl of seventeen, and had not been trained or prepared or educated as those astronauts were who went to the moon, she first experienced the enormous physical changes that occur in pregnancy.

How, I wondered, during those nauseous weeks, did she understand it? The aching breasts; the darkening aureolas. Her thickening hair; the stripe that appeared from her belly button down to her pelvis. How could she, a creature who never had a mother, have observed such physical changes with anything other than terror? What am I? she must have wondered. What kind of creature is this?

Or so I imagined, during those nauseous weeks, when I was trying to write a novel about Mary Shelley. She was a motherless girl, I thought, disowned by her father, when she gave birth for the first time. When she lost her baby after two weeks. When she got pregnant again. When she gave birth to her second baby.

Two parentless years, those were, of such rapid and incomprehensible shifts in physical and emotional state: and then another two years after that, when she gave birth to another baby, then lost both of her children to fever, then gave birth to a baby again. Three years later, she lost another pregnancy when she miscarried in Italy, and nearly bled to death, and then it was only a matter of weeks until her husband died. Then she was alone with her one remaining baby, with whom she returned to London. There, she started work on *The Last Man*, her final novel: a novel she described as autobiographical, though it is also a work of science fiction.

In it, she recasts the characters who were present that summer at Byron's villa—herself, Shelley, Byron, Claire, and John Polidori—as the last survivors of a pandemic who, together, create a happy Eden in the midst of disease, hunger, and violence. One by one, however, they die, until finally only the hero remains: a character whose life resembles Mary Shelley's.

Except that, in the book, she makes herself a man. And he is who she leaves alone, abandoned by his friends, consoled only by memories of a former happiness.

Actually, he's not alone. He has a little dog. A little dog, with whom he sets off on a journey by boat, in the hopes of finding another survivor on a less devastated continent.

THIS WAS THE gist of the biographical novel I tried to write in the weeks and months after the doctor confirmed my pregnancy, when it was very cold and I was still nauseous all day, and Alabama extended the law Texas had already passed by passing a law forbidding abortion in any case, including rape, including incest, no matter how dangerously old or ill the mother was, no matter how young the girl was who was pregnant.

Once again, at my feet, the little dog trembled. Another year of boxes for him, the little dog I once adopted after his first family had abandoned him. Once again, we left our houseplants behind. And then, because I'd taken a job there, we started to drive from Montana to Iowa.

WE WERE, IN some ways, retracing our steps, taking the same journey we'd taken the previous summer, but backward. This time, however, because of the unusual flooding, the entire state of South Dakota was underwater. A year before, when we'd driven out to Montana from New York, it was green fields forever until you reached the Badlands. This time it was silver lakes, as far as the eye could see, on both sides of the highway.

I kept expecting to see arcs sailing over the horizon. It was as though God had attempted to wipe clean our old, flawed civilization, but hadn't managed to do it completely. He'd left behind wind turbines and billboards; rest stops and imperfect people lining up to buy hard-boiled eggs in plastic pods.

Perhaps, then, we were waiting for him to finish the job. Somewhere outside Sioux City, I went into a rest stop to go to the bathroom and because my big pregnant body had become difficult to maneuver in a small stall, I accidentally dropped my phone in the toilet. I fished it out and it seemed to be fine, but later, in the hotel, I made the mistake of plugging it in and it died. Then, all at once, I lost all my contacts: all my old texts, all the exchanges with friends I'd left in other cities.

For a while, sitting by the pool at the Holiday Inn in Sioux City, a pool I could still sit in while people swarmed all around me without any fear of contagion, I felt depressed. I'd lost all the text message exchanges I'd been storing since I'd been married the first time in Texas; since I moved to New York; since I got married again. Since we left together to move to Montana.

But then I realized: it's fine. That door has closed. That whole time, I thought, is long gone. So are those places. That *country* is gone, I thought, remembering the silver lakes we drove through to get to Sioux City, remembering the lost ocean I'd heard in Las Vegas, feeling a bit like the last man setting off in his ship to find a new country.

Perhaps, I thought, that's what it is to be a pregnant woman in this country: to be the last man, setting off in his ship to find a new country. And the next morning, we set off again: me and my husband and our dog and the baby growing inside me. We drove through the fields of Iowa as though we were sailing across a green sea. We drove as though we'd come to a new planet. We drove as though we'd crossed from the real world into a dream, or from a dream into the real world, as though we'd stepped into the pages of some science-fictional novel.

Birth
2019

THAT'S WHERE MY NOVEL ENDED: WITH MARY SHELLEY AS the last man, setting out in a ship with her dog as her only companion.

It wasn't a very good novel. I threw it away. But even so, in the weeks and months after we arrived in Iowa City, where everything appeared to be fine, that feeling stayed with me: the feeling of lastness, the feeling of having disembarked from the old planet.

It stayed with me all through the final months of my pregnancy, when I was so enormous, I felt as though a spell had been cast, and I had been transformed into a different kind of animal. At night, I had dreams I'd given birth to a litter of piglets, dreams I'd given birth to a puppy. On the weekends, I decorated a room for her.

In school, at my new job, I was teaching a class on science fiction. We were reading *Frankenstein*. My students, all of them diligent and mature, far more diligent and mature than I was when I was in college, were discussing the ominous, science-fictional tone that runs through Victor Frankenstein's story: even in the beginning, when the monster hasn't yet been created, and Frankenstein is describing his happy family.

These students, who handed in stories about lonely characters on spaceships, living out their lives far away from a dead or dying planet, were saying how true to life this sense of dread is: how science-fictional real life in the twenty-first century can sometimes seem, what with the looming threats of global warming, the murderous gangs of police, the school shootings, the endless wars, the restrictions on reproductive rights.

And I was about to agree, to say how science-fictional life often seemed to me as well, when one of my best students raised their hand and said: But isn't there something unethical about imagining real life as science fiction? As though this is just a dream, or a story, or a prelude to the action with monsters? When in fact this is a real planet we're destroying, and real, living people we're hurting?

It's one thing, my student said, to invent science fiction to better understand our real lives. But isn't there something escapist about comparing real life with science fiction? Doesn't it not only encourage a certain useless and generalized dread, but also provide an excuse for avoidance? As when people talk about the multiverse, which always seems to be shorthand for saying that the decisions they make in this life don't have grave and final consequence?

So my student said, and all the other students agreed with them, and I realized this was yet another occasion where they had proven themselves more diligent and mature than I myself was. And I wanted to improve, I really did, but even so: when I walked home, pregnant and uncomfortable, following the banks of the Iowa River, a toxic river polluted by waste from the factory farms upstream, where, I had recently read, mother pigs gave birth in cages so small they couldn't move, and there was no straw for them to nest with their piglets, and no room for them to cuddle their piglets as pigs usually do, and their piglets were ripped away at three weeks, never again to see their mothers, I couldn't help but feel I was living in a world that wasn't quite natural.

The feeling stayed with me all through my walk home, and it was that night that a bat came into our house. I had finally fallen asleep, something that had become hard for me to do, because my body was so enormous and by then quite painful. There was always a sharp stabbing sensation just under my sternum, and my hips always ached, no matter how many pillows I placed between my knees, and so, though I was always tired, and always went to bed before my husband, I'd lie awake, and would still be awake when he came to bed and fell asleep as soon as he lay his head on the pillow.

But that night, unusually, I had finally fallen asleep and stayed asleep when my husband came in, and only woke when I heard a weird flapping. At first, I thought it was the window shade banging on the window frame, but then I got up to go fix it, and as I was standing at the window, I felt a fluttering around my head and my shoulder. I assumed it was a very large moth. And so I went back to bed, but, lying there, I realized that, for a moth, it had been heavy. And so I turned on the lamp, and there was a bat, hanging over the window.

For no reason at all, I started whimpering. I began to crouch down by the bed. Still, my husband was sleeping. Finally, I reached over and shook him. "There's a bat," I hissed, "by the window." Half rousing himself, he told me to go downstairs. Dumbly, with the body and the snout of a pregnant animal, I went downstairs and sat on the couch, and for a while I heard him moving around in the bedroom. There were several loud bangs. Then I heard him say, "Jesus fucking

Christ," and I was sure he'd killed the bat: I was sure there was bat blood all over our bedroom.

He came downstairs wearing a baseball hat and a hoodie and the frilled yellow cleaning gloves I'd recently bought at the grocery store. "It's still up there," he said.

He'd tried to catch it under the cleaning bucket, but it kept crawling out through the curved lip. "It was squeaking," he said. He was obviously shaken. Then he went upstairs again, and for a while there was more noise, more banging around. When he came downstairs, he announced that the bat had flown out the window.

Still, however, he felt we should go to the hospital to get rabies vaccines, because sometimes bat bites are very light, and people don't know they've been bitten. I felt this was absurd, so we called the hospital to ask a nurse, and she said it was true: sometimes people don't know they've been bitten, and there was an unusually high incidence of rabies in the bat community of Iowa City.

I went upstairs to get dressed. For a while, I rummaged around in the closet for sweatpants and socks, and when I turned around to come out, there was the bat: hanging over the closet door.

Suddenly, with absolute clarity, I realized this bat had bitten me. I knew that the bat had bitten and infected me, that every cell in my body had been infected with bat DNA, including the cells of my little bat baby. Then, just as suddenly, the terror that had been in me since I'd seen the bat—and, perhaps, now that I think about it, long before then—faded away. It was done. It was too late. Something had been shared between that bat and me.

Calmly, I crossed the threshold beneath him. In the bedroom, I opened the window. "Fly away," I told him, in no uncertain tone. Then I left the room, closing the door behind me. I had to trust he'd be gone when we came home from the hospital.

We spent that night in the emergency room, waiting for them to give us our shots, because first they had to confirm that the vaccine was safe for a woman in her third trimester. In the morning, when we finally left, it was light out. It was also fall. The day before, it had been hot. Now, suddenly, the season had changed. When we got home, I slept for a few hours in our sunny bedroom. I dreamed I gave birth to a bat. I dreamed I held in my arms a little bat baby. How grateful I felt: to be given such a lovely bat baby.

In the late morning, when I woke, I thought that perhaps it would be for the best: that in such a strange, violent world, a world in which the waters were rising, a world full of factory farms, maybe it would be best for my daughter to have some bat DNA. And I moved through the last days of my pregnancy a little relieved, unnaturally calm, and still unable to shake the suspicion that the world had tilted ever so slightly toward the science-fictional.

PERHAPS, THEN, I was ready to feel as though I'd departed from Earth when the day finally came that I went into labor.

It started around seven at night. The cramps were manageable at first, especially if I breathed through them as I had been taught in the childbirth class in the basement of Mercy Hospital, where they handed out clothespins to pinch your fingers so you could practice breathing through pain. Using my breathing techniques, I could easily manage those early cramps, and so, at that point, I still believed I might emerge from childbirth with grace and equanimity.

I had reason to believe this. The women in my family—I had always been told—have a high threshold for pain. My sister, for instance, had two children without epidurals. So did my mother. My mother was induced with Pitocin, a kind of labor most people believe is too painful to attempt without anesthesia. But, throughout my life, if I ever asked her if it hurt, she always shrugged and said something about how the women in our family have excellent pain tolerance.

And so, just after dinner, when the contractions began intensifying to the point that I could no longer ignore them, I felt a surge of ancestral womanly pride when I told my husband that labor had begun and that he should get some sleep. For a while, I even lay down beside him, proud of my grace, my maternal generosity.

But the contractions, when they came, were growing stronger and stronger. It was becoming difficult for me to breathe through them. Then I got out of bed and went downstairs in the darkness. There, it was just me and the little dog, alone in the living room, as it had been back in the days after my divorce, when I had unraveled my life, before I met my new husband, and it was just me and the dog in a series of strange and unpleasant apartments.

Then, as I had been taught to do, I lay on the couch with a pillow between my legs and tried to breathe. I counted the length of the contractions, and the time between the contractions. In the classes I had attended in the basement of Mercy, we had been told that we should come in when the contractions lasted longer than a minute, and the time between them was less than a minute. Then, feeling smug because of my family history, I had imagined that this early stage of labor wouldn't be a problem for me. Now, however, as I had been taught, I breathed through the pain and counted carefully, but the contractions had become extraordinarily painful. They felt as though someone had laced wires through and around my pelvis and were tightening the wires with levers, pulling apart the bones in my hips.

Or so I said to myself at the time, trying, in my state of pain and solitude, to find a way to describe it to myself: it was, I said to myself in the darkness, with the dog looking up at me from below, as though someone had laced wires through the bones of my pelvis.

And yet, even then, I realized that the description fell short: that the side of myself to whom I was describing my pain could not, in fact, understand it. And the awareness of my inability to describe what I was feeling only served to compound the helplessness of the experience, so that even in the minutes between the contractions, minutes when I wasn't in pain, I lay there in the living room and felt as though I'd been exiled to a new kind of aloneness.

Between contractions, trying to focus on something other than waiting for the next contraction to start, I looked at the bookshelves. There was nothing to see, nothing there that could possibly help me. All those books were meaningless now, though on so many other occasions I had turned to them for assistance. But now, I realized, they were useless to address the state I was in, utterly helpless to help me, except perhaps one, a slim gray spine I looked for and found: *The Body in Pain*, that famous book by Elaine Scarry, a book I'd been assigned to read in college and hadn't thought about since, though I'd toted it with me for centuries, moving it between so many apartments.

This was something she'd talked about. Pain, she'd written, is defined by its refusal to be expressed. Its refusal to be expressed is essential to what it is. In fact, she said, if pain *can* be expressed, it becomes something other than pain. And if other states of consciousness (loneliness, for instance, or fear) cannot find a way to express themselves, they will be nothing other than painful.

Sitting there in the darkness of the living room, I remembered the metaphor Elaine Scarry used. In pain, she said, we are stranded in a void of inexpressibility: a void so unimaginable to other people that it resembles the farthest-flung distances of outer space.

Yes, I thought, finding the small gray spine of that book on the shelf, a spine that seemed to have detached itself from the other spines, and was now floating in the darkness while the contraction ramped up. Yes, that's what it was. I was heading into space. Time had begun to lengthen in strange and unpredictable ways. The contractions, which had become so painful I couldn't even describe them to myself, as you can't explain pain to an animal, or an animal can't explain pain to itself, were getting long. Often, they lasted longer than a minute, and yet they never came less than a minute apart, so I told myself it wasn't yet time to wake up my husband.

By then, I was still trying to breathe through the contractions, but it was growing harder and harder, and most of the time I ended up giving up on such breathing, and instead clawed my leg with my nails in the attempt to distract myself from the greater pain of the contraction.

Then the contraction faded, but I felt somehow changed by it, or the living room seemed to have been changed, and the book still hung in the air. In the same book, I remembered, the same book with its little gray spine, I had read that pain can feel different depending on the meaning we give it: that pain in childbirth—a pain we can feel proud of—may cause less pain than the pain of a violence inflicted upon us.

But the pain I felt, during those early contractions: it didn't cause me to feel proud. I was ashamed, in fact, of how much I was feeling it. It seemed to me that if I had the right kinds of motherly feelings—the right kind of love, the right kind of strength, the right spirit of self-sacrifice—I wouldn't be feeling this as pain at all.

Perhaps, I realized, I did not have a high threshold for pain. Perhaps my pain threshold was low. It was possible, I realized, that I lacked the strength I'd assumed was mine as a woman who came from my family, a family of women who survived worse than labor, a family of women who passed through something as simple as labor in a few merely uncomfortable hours. It was possible, I realized during the minutes between the lengthening contractions, contractions that were now always over two minutes, that I was not such a woman. It was possible, in fact, that I might not get through this.

This stage of the contractions—which often lasted three or four minutes but never occurred less than a minute apart—continued not for twenty minutes or so, but for one hour, then another, then another four. By then, the repeated barrages of pain, punctuated by periods of calm in which I waited tensely for the pain to return, were causing me to begin to feel somewhat frantic. Around one a.m., I called the hospital and asked if I could come in.

I felt I needed a person to help me. The nurse, however, held the line strictly. She told me not to come in until the contractions were less than a minute apart. She suggested that I take a hot bath. I clutched the counter and waited for the next contraction to end, then, obedient, went upstairs and ran a bath and lay alone in the tub—so far from my sleeping husband by then that it was clear that we lived on different planets—and tried not to cry out in the darkness, or to pull the shower curtain down off the rod when a contraction started and lasted three, four, sometimes five or six minutes.

When I got out of the bath, I woke my husband up. I told him we were going to the hospital. Then I called the hospital again. I told the same nurse that the contractions lasted five or six minutes, but that they still weren't coming less than a minute apart. She was clearly unimpressed when I told her how strong the contractions were and how long they lasted, since on the other hand they still weren't coming that close. This was the same phone call she received every night. She suggested I take another bath. My husband stumbled back to bed. The space between us yawned. I reeled. The dog, concerned, looked up at me.

I ran another bath. We had run out of hot water, so the bath was lukewarm, and it didn't help me at all. Not, at least, in the ways baths seemed to help the women in the videos they showed us in childbirth classes at Mercy, videos of calm women who breathed through the pain, then smiled up at their spouses.

When the next contraction passed, I got out of the cold water, dripping and slicked like a monster emerging out of the sea. I bared my teeth at the wall. I cursed my husband; I cursed the nurse. Then I dressed again. I went back down to the couch. There, the contractions came hard enough that it was too hard to try to breathe through them, and so instead I gritted my teeth and clawed at my leg, or the fabric on the couch.

Below me, fearing the worst, the dog trembled wildly. You could see the whites of his eyes. His whole body was quaking. I tried to reassure him, then thought about my husband sleeping. I thought about Mary Shelley at seventeen, giving birth to her first baby, later leaving the continent with no one but a little dog on her ship. Do you ever emerge, I asked her in my mind, from this utter aloneness?

Around three in the morning, having discarded the idea that I would get through this experience with any grace, I woke my husband again. I told him we were going to the hospital. Then I called the nurse. She told me not to. Then, once again, I lost my nerve, and my husband went back to sleep, and once again it was me and the dog alone in the darkness of the most distant galaxies, the dog looking up at me, me on my side, trying to breathe, but often becoming frantic as the pain of the contractions lasted for eight and sometimes nine minutes, a pattern that continued until finally, around five in the morning, my water broke: a sudden blast of hot liquid wetness that soaked my pants so that I got up and rushed to the bathroom assuming with a great wave of shame that the pain of the contractions had caused me to wet myself, only to turn on the bathroom light to find a pool of bloody water all over the floor, a terrifying pool, much bloodier than anything I'd imagined when they told us in the basement about how our "water" might "break."

Our water? No. Our body, our blood. Everything inside us might break, blow, burn against the bounds of us, flood over our shores.

For a moment, looking down at that enormous bloody pool on the tile, I wondered whether, in fact, I'd given birth but there was no baby. I clutched the sink. The dog, outside the bathroom door, was wide-eyed and convulsing in terror. I had given birth to no baby.

I knew that, for sure, in that moment. Then my reason kicked in. I realized that it was more likely that my water had broken, so I went upstairs and woke my husband again, because I'd been told to go to the hospital as soon as my water broke, even if I still wasn't having contractions. As I went up the stairs, however, I was followed by a bloody trail, one that made me feel shame, and so even though my husband had already rushed out to the car—now, for some reason, he was suddenly rushing—I was stooping to mop up the blood on the stairs with the pants I'd changed out of, until finally my husband rushed in again and begged me to stop, and we drove over the river in darkness.

EVERYONE ALWAYS TELLS you that you will forget. That amnesia sets in; that afterward, you're so happy and in love that you immediately forget your former agony.

I, however, remember labor. I remember being helped into the hospital room, everyone rushing, as though something might happen quickly. I remember changing into my gown. I remember the next contraction that hit, and the way I thought about something my sister had told me: that it helped to imagine the pain as waves in the ocean, each wave washing over you.

I remember trying to imagine the pain as a purifying wave of water, and I remember how, instead, I noted that the pain seemed to scrape against the rusting bowl of my pelvis. There was one happy moment when the nurse measured my dilation and praised me for how much labor I'd done at home, so that, though I clearly wasn't handling this with the superiority and self-abnegation I'd once imagined would be mine, I did, for a moment, feel proud. And then that pride was eliminated once again by a new wave of pain, which I handled poorly, followed by another moment of pride when they connected me to a machine that measured the intensity and length of the contractions and informed me—as though for the first time—that they were unusually strong and unusually long. But then it was also true that the time between contractions was also abnormally long, and so they hooked me up to a Pitocin drip to try to speed up the labor, which didn't work, at least not right away, and only served to intensify the pain associated with each one of the endless contractions.

AND EVEN SO: there were stretches of minutes between contractions, periods of emptiness in which I had time to think.

That pain, for instance: What was the purpose of it? What was I learning from feeling that pain? What was I coming to know? Did feeling it allow me to be more present as my child came into the world? Did it cause me to be more alert to that precious experience?

Many women I knew, when I was pregnant, talked about the benefits of "natural" birth, of birth they had managed without anesthesia. Several women, indeed, had—unbidden—gifted me books on how to manage birth without anesthesia, books that explained why a natural birth was better both for the mother and for the baby.

Pregnant, round, and with my obedient snout, I read those books and believed them, but sometimes, reading those passages about finding peace in the pain, or feeling the blessing of your child coming, I found it annoying to think how closely their message aligned with the message of Christian doctors in nineteenth-century Europe and America, doctors who believed, even after the discovery of anesthetic, that pain was a curse God gave to women, a punishment for their sin, their criminal desire for knowledge, and that therefore they should still labor through it.

Back then, it was believed that women could bear more pain than men. It was believed that, if they screamed, it was not because they couldn't stand the pain they'd been given, but because women expressed pain more volubly than men did. No one believed, when they were denying women anesthetic for religious reasons, that the pain they felt in labor might be too much for their minds to bear. Not the loneliness of that pain; not the chaos of it. No one believed that the depressions women sometimes sank into in the months after their babies were born were the result of those long stretches of pain in which they'd been absolutely abandoned.

Such beliefs may have been left behind by mainstream medicine, and yet, still, here were these experts publishing books, recommending that women should not only bear the pain of labor, but feel grateful for the gift of it. Pregnant, I read those books and believed them, and when I got to the hospital, I told the nurse I didn't want an epidural. No: I wanted to give birth naturally. I did not meditate on the fact that there were already many aspects of the birth that were not perfectly natural: the hospital, the Pitocin, the antibiotics, the IV drips. No: that did not factor into my thinking, when I refused the nurse who offered me an epidural. Perhaps, then, it had less to do with naturalness and more to do with my desire to prove myself to be a certain kind of person, a certain kind of mother, one who could suppress her own pain, one who could be silent in the face of suffering, one who did not too volubly express a growing agony.

As a result, when the contractions heightened, amplified by the stream of Pitocin that was pumping directly into my veins, I tried not to scream. The contractions, however, were quite horribly painful. Still, however, I declined the nurse's offer to call the anesthesiologist. When each new contraction started to rise, I began to brace myself for the pain, and my husband hauled himself out of the armchair and dutifully attempted—as he'd been instructed in the childbirth class we'd attended in the basement—to massage my lower back with his thumbs.

How useless they were, his efforts to help! Sometimes, in the midst of his hideously failing attempts, I tried to give him instructions he did not understand and so continued getting it wrong and not helping, so that the pain that was also loneliness and now rage continued to rear up in my body.

It reared up higher and higher, becoming more wretched with each passing minute, and now also I had him fumbling around at my back, fumbling around and not understanding, the least understanding person alive on the planet, something I had to bear in addition to the pain which was still increasing, so that as I tried to bear it I grew increasingly frantic, and finally somewhat lunatic, and several times ended up reaching back and hitting him, shoving him or punching his forearm over and over again, like a dog who gets hit by a car and then bites the first person who tries to help him.

And, indeed, speaking of dogs: sometimes, when the contraction had passed, and my husband had sunk back into his chair in utter stupefied blankness, I'd look at him in pure fury and think that the dog, at home, had been more helpful. I'd wish it was the dog who had come with me: the dog, who did not try to help, who did not try to do anything to alleviate my suffering, but only huddled there with me, his whole body trembling. His was the species to which I now belonged. Or so I thought, as the contractions subsided, and my husband returned to his armchair and rested.

SO THE ENDLESS morning progressed. Hours and hours of this, being told that while the contractions were unusually long and intense, the time between them was still too expansive, and dilation wasn't progressing, and so waiting, then punching my husband, then waiting again for the next wave of pain, and, when it came, and as it built, growing more and more violently and viciously frantic.

And then the lulls, during which I could think. What, I kept asking myself between the contractions, was the point? What was the point of feeling this? If it was a test of my ability to set myself aside, I felt myself to be failing it. My self, my wretched self and its failures: that was all I was concerned with. If that pain was meant to make me present for the birth of my child, or if that pain was meant to allow me to know my own strength, or if that pain was meant to cause me to know what other women have felt, and so bind me to other mothers, it failed to accomplish its point, and only caused me to feel frantic. It caused me to feel a frantic, evil loneliness: a crazed and somewhat hysteric resentment toward every other person around, since I alone had been cast off into this darkness.

No one, no one on Earth had come with me. I had been exiled to space. How they all stood there and watched while I spiraled off.

Oh, how I hated them. I hated them all, when I finally asked for my epidural.

TWO HOURS LATER, when the anesthesiologist arrived, the nurse, recognizing that I was losing my mind, asked my husband to get out of the way. Then she stood behind me and restrained me herself, and I was in her strong arms when the anesthesiologist inserted the long needle into my spine and hit what she later called a "nerve center."

Or, perhaps (it would not have been easy for me to know the difference), the needle hit at the most intense moment of a contraction, and, in that moment, I simply lost the last shreds of my remaining sanity. I can't really be sure; they didn't know, either. Afterward, they debated the fact. All that was clear was that, when the needle hit, I started screaming in a way that must have terrified the anesthesiologist as well as the nurse, because between them they made the decision to abort the procedure.

Therefore, unanesthetized, still hysterical, I went back to labor, and the contractions still weren't coming fast enough, and the dilation wasn't happening fast enough, but I didn't want to risk the horror of attempting another epidural. And so the pain increased, now less of a physical pain and more of an increasing terror that was ramping up to lunacy.

The nurse who had been with me went home to sleep. A new nurse came in. She tried to soothe me. Yes, she said, breathe. It will help to focus on the crucifix. There it was: hanging on the wall in direct view, though slightly askew, so that it looked like an X, another planet's crucifix. The unknown in a problem I couldn't solve. She wanted me to focus on that. She meant that it would help me get through the contractions if I bent my mind to something outside my own body. And then I did, or tried, but it was hard to keep my mind on anyone's pain but my own, and so I turned from him again, and still the contractions were spaced too far apart, and still when they did come, they were unendurably long, and I realized I'd have much preferred nails through my hands than those hideously increasing contractions. By then, they had adjusted the Pitocin to the highest possible dose, and when, around two, in my fury, in my pure rage, I did finally ask to try an epidural again, they told me it would be another two hours before the anesthesiologist could come back.

He had gone, they said, to the other hospital.

WHAT ABSOLUTE ABSURDITY! What an utterly, crazily, stupid state of affairs. As though anesthesiologists traveled by mule between the village hospitals. It was as though my pain had caused me to travel back several centuries. And so, utterly at the end of my rope, a mule at the end of her tether, I asked if there was anything else they could do, and they told me they could give me a medicine that would not eliminate the pain, but would cause me not to care that I felt it.

So that's what I did. And indeed, as soon as I had taken it, I still felt the same painful sensations, but I no longer cared.

I didn't care the least bit. Within minutes, I was entirely reconciled and in love with my husband, pleased even to the point of laughing along with him about how lovely it was not to care, how extraordinary it was to know that pain didn't matter, that pain didn't *exist*, as long as we didn't care that we felt it.

Everything was so smooth, so perfectly easy, that it seemed to me I was dreaming. That perhaps my body was still in space, but I was finally sleeping, and now, in my dreams, I had returned to Earth and my family. As time moves in dreams, so time moved for me then: smoothly, without ever catching on difficult minutes, one hour melting into the next so that you can dream a whole week in the course of ten minutes of sleep, or two hours can pass and you can care not in the least while you wait for the village anesthesiologist.

WHEN HE DID finally come, and pulled out his needle, he started singing. He was singing a carefree little song while he pushed his needle into my spine. Looking back on that song, I realize he believed it would calm me, since, as soon as he pulled his needle out of his case, my whole body had begun shaking.

But it was shaking without me. I myself was perfectly calm. I was aware that I might feel, once again, the same extraordinary pain I'd felt the last time the needle went in. But this time, I didn't care. Nor did I care when the epidural went smoothly.

Then, for a few hours, I slept. When I woke, my husband was asleep in his armchair. Then I called my mother, who had flown in the previous night and was staying in a nearby hotel. I asked her to come see me. When she arrived, we chatted for a while, my mother and I, or she visited me in a dream. I was drinking apple juice. She'd brought me a tube of the right kind of ChapStick. Her hair—my mother's hair—smelled like fall leaves.

In the dream, while my husband slept, my mother was talking about various things—where, for instance, she and my father would live if they sold their house in California—and I was thinking about how painless this was, when suddenly I began to suspect that I wasn't actually giving birth to a baby.

It was then—though I couldn't say this to my mother; as

in any dream, I couldn't just speak when I wanted to speak—
that the dream began to feel scary. I realized, then, in the
dream, that there wasn't a baby inside me. This, I began to
understand, was another unreal pregnancy. The reason, I finally saw, for the strange length of time between the contractions was the fact that I was actually empty.

In the dream, I wanted to say this to my mother, who
herself gave birth to a dead baby. But it was as though my
mouth wouldn't open. She was talking about where she
would move with my father, the fires and the floods, her fear
of mortality, and my mouth couldn't open to scream.

Then my mother went out for more apple juice to bring
to her daughter, and my husband was still asleep, and there I
lay, unable to wake from this terrible dream. Unable to speak;
unable to tell anyone that now I was frightened, and realizing with utter certainty that when the time came to push, the
nurses and the doctors would realize I was actually empty.

Then, for the first time, I began to see it all clearly: that
the pain, in fact, was the distraction. The pain was the crucifix, meant to distract me from comprehending emptiness.

And then my mother returned, and we talked about
whether she wanted to move to a new city, or simply move to
a new house in the same city, though the droughts were so bad
it had grown prohibitively expensive to water the garden. But
where could she move? She loved California, she had gotten
too old for another long winter, and so on and so forth, but
the whole time I trembled, knowing my inner emptiness.

Then, finally, the nurse came and told me it was time for
me to push. My husband woke and held my hand, and, for a
while, I pushed. It didn't hurt. And it wasn't hard. It was, in

fact, so painless and easy that I knew a baby was not really coming. I knew, in fact, that I was perfectly empty. Until, suddenly, they gathered her up. And placed her on my chest: a small, surprising, gray, slippery baby.

DID ALL THAT really happen? It must have happened on the moon. That night, we were alone, the baby and I, in a hospital room on a new planet. Her brow was a furrow. And when she opened her mouth to cry: the darkness within it was an estuary, and behind it a river that tunneled deep into her planet's center. All night, I sat with her and nursed her, and through the window I could see the chalked shape of the earth far away in the night sky.

Her forehead was petal-soft. Her hands were impossibly small, just the size to cling to a finger. At my breast, she sucked, all through the night, and, in the morning, when she opened her eyes for the first time, they were so shining and dark it was clear they'd been hewn straight from the sky of the farthest galaxy.

This little girl: she learned to nurse quickly, and even when she fell asleep she was still sucking. Holding this girl, asleep and still sucking, I asked the night sky: Was she mine? No, she was the moon's. It was important to hold this moon baby gently.

WHO COULD SAY how the nurse got to the moon, to give me instructions for bathing this baby, and to tell me what to do, if, in the upcoming days, I started bleeding heavily?

Sitting there, cheerful, with her hair pulled back in an enormous ribbon, she picked up an empty apple juice bottle. If a clot of blood, she said, the size of this bottle should come out of your body, that is an organ. Then you should come back to the hospital.

Hearing this, my mother—she, too, was there on the moon—began to laugh. All day, she kept hysterically laughing. She simply couldn't let the joke go: an organ the size of an apple juice bottle. If an organ comes out of your body, she kept saying, wiping away tears of laughter, you better head back to the hospital.

All this happened on the moon, and later, my husband and I emerged from the hospital with our baby into a world that was so bright and crisp and burnished it was as though we were wandering through a film we'd seen once about autumn, as though we'd hallucinated this autumn day and this baby, and then an old friend of my husband's, someone I'd never met, drove by and stopped, and, holding our baby, I couldn't hear what she was saying from within her car, chatting about this and that and languidly waving a cigarette.

We were still dreaming on the moon a week later, a hundred thousand miles from Earth and everyone on it, alone now because my mother had climbed aboard her ship and headed back to the old planet, when in the middle of a bright and shining gold afternoon I started bleeding, and kept bleeding so hard—all over the bathroom floor, all over my hands and my arms, pools of blood and also clots, coin-sized clots, then clots the size of clementines, two of which I carried downstairs to show my husband, and said, *Is this natural, am I meant to be bleeding this heavily?*—that we strapped our baby into the car seat and drove back to the emergency room.

There, I bled and bled, all over the waiting room floor, all over the floor of the room they finally gave me to bleed in, though for some reason no one could help stop the bleeding, or explain to me why I was bleeding, and instead an elfin orderly with bleached hair simply came in every twenty minutes or so to change my gown and all the bedding and mop up the pools of blood on the floor, the clots of blood on the linoleum, many of which were bigger than a bottle of apple juice, so that at one point in my terror I picked one up and said, *Is this an organ?* and the orderly told me she didn't know, to set it down on the table for later.

And later a doctor came in to inspect it, then left because I was nursing the baby, though as he was heading out, I pleaded with him to stay. Later, he returned and examined the clot. He wondered whether or not to perform an ultrasound, then left, and later came back to order an ultrasound that found nothing. Then I went back to waiting and bleeding and I had begun uncontrollably shivering. Now the baby was crying, she wanted to nurse again, and while she nursed, I was so cold I began to beg for a blanket, but no one seemed able to find one. They could only send the elfin orderly, who looked like she could be no older than twelve, to mop up the blood that had pooled underneath me. Did I imagine that, when she was finished, she bent close to my ear and whispered, *My sister went through this, I helped her get through this*? I recall that she said that. Then she left with her mop, and I remained in the room, bleeding, one hour passing into the next, until finally someone thought to transfer me to the maternity wing, where at least the nurses seemed to know what to do, and with prompt and absolute authority hooked me up to an IV drip of medicine they told me they hoped might slow down the bleeding.

Then the nurses began to push hard on my abdomen every ten minutes, and to catch the blood clots that poured out in plastic bags, which they carried over to a scale to weigh, in the hopes that the bleeding was slowing.

But it didn't slow. It didn't slow in the hours after they put me on that medicine, nor did it slow when they put me on a drip of Pitocin in order to induce labor contractions that they hoped would slow the hemorrhage. Then, once again, I found myself breathing through the contractions, one hour lurching into the next, but this time I was also nursing a baby, and each time they massaged my abdomen I felt clotted blood sliding out of my body. By then, I was so violently shivering that the metal hospital cot was rattling.

My husband, trying to keep me warm, climbed into bed with me, so I clung to him, just as I clung to our baby. And when the next contraction came, I gritted my teeth, and the nurse who was pressing my abdomen gestured toward the crucifix, and I realized that now, in fact, I was giving birth but there was no baby. That the waking dream—or waking nightmare—that had come to me while I was in labor had become reality.

And so on and so forth, all through that night and well into the next morning, when the bleeding still hadn't slowed. When, every ten minutes, the nurses were still carrying bags of blood over to the scale, and inserting more needles to take blood to run tests on, though by then they had used up all the easy veins on my arms and hands and wrists, so they used the webs between my fingers, the veins in my ankles, and it seemed clear to me that nothing was working.

Nothing was working and nothing would work to stop the bleeding, and here was my little baby, stolen from the moon, here now, and determinedly nursing. Shivering, I held my moon baby and listened while the doctor told the nurse to prepare for surgery.

THIS, TO BE honest, was something of a shock: I hadn't been aware that surgery was an option. No one had explained that to me. I had simply believed I was dying.

And so, when the doctor turned from the nurse and told me that the Bakri balloon might not work at this point, and asked me if I would consent to a hysterectomy, if I could accept not having any more babies, it was a somewhat confusing and even painful question, as though someone had asked me to imagine some other version of my life in which I had survived, some other version in which I had gotten to stay and live with my baby.

As though the doctor had asked me, a dying woman: Would that living woman mind not having more babies? On that woman's behalf I gave my consent, and so, with that in mind, they began to prepare to wheel me to the operating theater, and the one baby I did have—who seemed to be instructing me in the kind of persistence required for a human being to keep living—nursed one more time, determinedly, with her little brow furrowed, before they finally wheeled me away.

Away I went, down one hall, then another, into an elevator, down another long hallway, all of them perfectly empty, all those hallways abandoned, as though a plague had spread through the hospital, as though a hurricane had sent every last person away, as though I were getting wheeled through a dream that had become reality.

Somewhere, I thought, in a boat, the little dog must be waiting for me.

It was then, finally, that they wheeled me through doors I somehow recognized, and into a cold clean room, a room that looked like a morgue, or a clean meat locker in a grocery store, another dream I had made real, and someone was holding my hand, and someone else gave me a mask and I breathed and began again to go under.

I CAME TO in another waiting room. Someone gave me a wax paper cup full of ice and told me the balloon had stopped the hemorrhage before I bled out. For some reason, I'd lost my voice, or forgotten how to use my throat, so I gestured to her for another cup of ice. I scooped with my paw; I listened to my teeth crunching. And then there was another room where I received the blood transfusions. And later, too, another dark room where I was told to pump with the hospital breast pump to rid myself of the milk that was now toxic with various types of anesthetic. There, an old woman sat beside me, flipping through an enormous book of chemicals and how long they last in breast milk. When the pump arrived, wheeled in by an orderly, a pump the size of the kind you use to pump gas into a vehicle, the old woman showed me how to press the flanges over my nipples, watched while the bottles filled up with milk, held the bottles up to the light and sighed, Oh, oh, how I hate to waste it.

Then she left me in the darkness, and for an hour or two, I was meant to sleep, but kept worrying, wide-eyed, about how my moon child was surviving. Then, finally, they wheeled me into another room, where my husband was holding the baby, who was crying wildly. Finally, I held her, and she nursed, drinking the milk that I had been promised was clean. My husband drew the curtains aside. While I'd been in surgery, it had started snowing. The roofs of all the hospital buildings were white, and the trees, and the white sky had lowered above them.

*Beautiful, beautiful*, Buzz Aldrin said when he joined Neil Armstrong on the surface of the moon: *magnificent desolation*. So it was, on that day, looking through the hospital window.

And several days later, when I emerged from the hospital, and climbed into the car with my husband and our baby, the world was silent and white. Silent and white, when we drove over the river again, silent and white when we drove past the park, where drifts of snow that glittered like moondust were swept over the whiteness by passing gusts. Silent, and white, when the three of us emerged from the car, alone on the moon, the two of us and our little baby.

THERE, ALL THROUGH the winter, we lived together in a house that had become the whole world. Yes, even then, even in those three months before the quarantine had begun, our house on the moon had become the whole world, a warmed and heated pod in the midst of an inhospitable environment. All day the snow fell, but I lived at night, nursing the baby, walking with her in the darkness to keep her from crying. When she finally slept, her body small and weighty and warm as a cat's, she was a creature I barely recognized. When she woke, she stared at me with eyes hewn from distant galaxies.

Sometimes, at night, to keep myself awake while I nursed, I read the news about the virus in Wuhan, and saw pictures of that empty city, snow swirling around empty highways: that moonscape of an abandoned city, a lunatic city, a moon-blind city, then read about how the virus had spread to Japan and South Korea. Then it had spread in those cruise ships, and then Iran and Italy, until finally we understood that it was also spreading in our own country.

And so we went into quarantine, and the world continued to recede, the world in which people couldn't bury their dead, the world in which the funeral parlor across from our old apartment in New York had begun to send bodies upstate to be stored until the cremation facilities could accept them. A world in which fires burned through the West, a world in which the police continued to murder, all so wretched, and so far away, these tragedies that occurred on the planet we'd left. Alone, then, the three of us, in our new spaceship, in a solitude in which we were the last remaining survivors, in which I stood holding my child at the window at night, and watched while deer moved slowly through the front garden as though I were watching strange bodies float past the window of the spaceship.

Then, from the distance of space, I thought about the old planet. Sometimes, at night, after nursing the baby, I'd look out at the sky and see the earth: rolling off toward the horizon. Our old distant, hazy, blue-and-green planet. From that perspective, I remembered how much I loved it.

Then, transported away, what love I had in my heart. Such love I felt, when I paced through the night on that other planet. From such a distance, I recalled even more clearly each tumbling green bough of each elm in the city. The scent of the fall we'd just lost: apples rotting and leaves getting wet. The sound of those geese, leaving that lake in Montana: gunmetal gray, snow-swept, and otherwise silent.

# Science Fiction

2021

# 1.

I BEGAN MY own Frankenstein story—my own offspring of happy days—in the fall of 2021, some months after I first re-united with my old friend Anna. It was June when she called me out of the blue, and I was pregnant for the third time.

Perhaps it was that strange, altered state—the nausea, the weariness, the silence and secrecy of early pregnancy—or perhaps it was the quarantine we'd remained in for over a year, or perhaps it was the still-lingering effects of my experi-ence giving birth, that made me want to write such a story: for, like Walton, the sea captain who tells Frankenstein's story in letters, I felt like something of an Arctic explorer in the days when Anna contacted me.

Like Walton when he encounters Frankenstein in the Arctic, I felt like a person alone, surrounded by vistas of white space. And the more I thought about Anna in this light, the more I realized she was a Frankenstein of sorts, a woman Frankenstein of the twenty-first century. That I was Walton and that Anna was Frankenstein, and that we were mirrors of each other, became clear to me that summer Anna reen-tered my life, and so a novel began to take shape in my mind, a new version of Mary Shelley's story, though it wasn't until Anna left, and much had changed in my own life, that I sat down and started to write it.

# 2.

I WAS SURPRISED when Anna called me. We hadn't talked for some time; I hadn't seen her since before the birth of my daughter. For a moment, when I saw her name on my phone, I felt frightened. Then I shook my head, annoyed at myself, and picked up. For reasons she said were too complicated to explain on the phone, she had moved from Austin to Iowa City, and she had something exciting she wanted to tell me.

We made plans to meet outside, at a coffee place on the pedestrian mall that sold drinks out of a window. I brought my daughter, and we headed out early so she could play on the playground while I waited for Anna.

As soon as I got her strapped into the stroller, however, I regretted having made plans to meet. For one thing, I was so nauseous. The nausea that comes with pregnancy is, for me, an absolutely isolating state. If, pregnant, you tell people you're nauseous, most of them will glow, and tell you it's a good sign. They'll tell you it's for a good cause. These people have never felt nauseous; certainly, they haven't felt nauseous while carrying a dead baby.

When you are actually nauseous, there is little room in your life for anything other than nausea. In the three periods of nausea that had occupied my life since I'd begun to try to get pregnant, periods that, combined, amounted to a year, I had cut everyone I knew out of my life so that I could focus on being nauseous. This time, this third time, it had been easier to remove myself, since I lived in a city where I still knew very few people, and we were in the middle of an ongoing pandemic.

It was for the best. Nauseous as I was, I didn't want to be around other people. It was all I could manage to try to be present and alive during those hours when I was with my daughter. To watch her at the playground, climbing the stairs: something she did with every part of her body, using not only her hands and her knees for leverage, but also her belly, her cheek, and even her forehead.

Watching her, from time to time, the nausea would subside. But then it would slide over the world again, burying it deep, so that, once again, all I could feel was terrible dread, dread and awful seasickness, and that's how I felt that morning, while I pushed my daughter downtown, and regretted making the decision to meet up with Anna.

All I wanted was to be left alone with my daughter. When we'd reached the ped mall, I'd helped her out of the stroller. Now she was circling the playground, pointing, calling, "Twash twash twash." She was obsessed with picking up litter. Alien as she still was, with another planet's native generosity, she hadn't yet learned that you are meant to leave litter for other people to clean.

While I watched her from the bench, she picked up a dented Coke can, a plastic bag, and several cigarette butts, then toddled them over to the black metal trash can. Each time she disposed of a piece of trash, she brushed her hands off, the universal human signal for having successfully completed a task. That much she had learned during her months on the planet. Then she went back to work, and under another bench she found a plastic cup half-full of hot beer. She was carrying it with both hands toward the trash can.

In every cell of my body, the nausea spilled over. "Baby," I called, "careful." She looked at me, perplexed, a little annoyed, to have the rhythm of her work interrupted, then continued carrying the cup to the trash can. I scanned the ped mall. No sign of Anna. She was five minutes late. I was tempted to take my daughter and leave. We still had time to head to the Museum of Natural History.

Why, I wondered, had I agreed to meet Anna? I wasn't even sure I liked her. She was a friend from the years when I lived in Texas: the years of my first marriage, before my divorce. I'd lived seven lives since then. That first life, a life I had believed was my own for eight or nine years, now seemed like a movie I'd seen once: a movie in which I'd played a small and somewhat forgettable part.

Anna, too, had played a small role. In the group of friends I'd had when I lived there, friends who were really friends of my ex-husband's, she'd been unique in that she was a scientist. The rest of them were aspiring artists. She was only part of the group because her boyfriend was a singer in a psychedelic folk band.

Because she was a biochemist, she was treated as something of an exotic specimen. Everyone talked about how brilliant she was. She had, in addition, startlingly blue eyes, set in a harsh, angular, face. There were already lines under her eyes, and lines from her mouth down to her cheeks; her skin was aging in the rapid way of people with pale skin and light freckles. Even so, however, among that group of friends, she was considered beautiful, but I sometimes suspected it was only because the standards of beauty were different if you were a biochemist, just as the standards of brilliance were different if you were the only scientist in a group of aspiring artists.

Though her face was severe, her personality was flat. In general, she seemed somewhat stoned, and often she was, so you never felt as though you really knew her. Of all the women in that group, she was the one I'd felt least close to, though there were years when we saw each other at shows nearly every weekend, and she and her boyfriend and my ex-husband and I, along with a few other couples, spent several long weekends in West Texas together.

Later, after my divorce, we'd become closer. But, looking back, as I did when I was waiting there by the playground on the pedestrian mall, it seemed clear that the closeness we'd had for a couple of years was born out of convenience more than anything else. When my ex-husband and I had gotten divorced, the rest of our friends had been either trying to get pregnant or having babies. I started resenting them all, with their contentment, their achievement, the completion of their lives. With their bellies, which seemed to grow into planets they lived on alone with their babies.

Only Anna wasn't planning on getting pregnant. She and her boyfriend had never gotten married. They'd had, from the beginning, something of a fraught relationship. It was known that he cheated on her all the time. We all assumed that she knew. But she never talked with any of us about it, never pulled anyone aside to confess her discontent; she just maintained her usual placid, stoned silence.

It was true that there were a few years when Anna got very thin, so thin you could see new lines on her face. Then she stopped coming out as much as she once had. Even then, however, when you did see her out, she was calm. If she was having strong feelings, she never gave vent to them.

By the time I was getting divorced, Anna and her boyfriend had broken up and gotten back together four or five times. He'd move out of the house they shared, and we all assumed that she paid for. Then he'd move in with some young, admiring fan of the band. Then things would change, and he'd move back in with Anna again.

The whole thing had, in fact, become fairly torturous. There had been a period, for instance, when another girl moved in with them. She was the drummer in a new band that Anna's boyfriend had started. Later, the drummer moved out again, and it was just Anna and her boyfriend for a while, and it seemed as though things had gotten better for them, when suddenly Anna moved out of their house and found herself another apartment. She'd been there a few months when I separated from my ex-husband.

# 3.

SITTING THERE AT the playground, watching my daughter climbing the stairs, feeling as though everything other than my daughter and my nausea were entirely unreal, but willing myself nevertheless to remember how I'd known Anna in the first place, I wondered whether there had ever been anything real between me and Anna.

After I separated from my ex-husband, the two of us often went out together. Once, at one of those bars on the east side with an ugly outdoor patio that was actually a parking lot strung up with lights, when Anna was less stoned than usual and quite a bit more drunk, she told me the whole story of her relationship with her ex-boyfriend.

They'd known each other, she told me, since college. She'd just arrived in New York when she met him. She'd been a child. She was so lonely without her family, so overwhelmed by the city, and then there he was, with all his knowledge. He was two years older than her, and so confident in the way he moved through the city. In some ways, he seemed like an extension of the place, but an extension she could know and lie next to, a piece of it that she could appeal to.

From the very beginning, Anna told me, she'd been in love. But he was hard to get close to. One night he'd be in bed with her, and he'd have such sweetness: he'd sing silly songs; he'd pretend he was a scary monster. Like a child, he'd fall asleep with his arms around her. The next night, gone cold, he'd avoid her at a party. She'd feel as though he'd murdered her. The whole thing, she said, was so perplexing. He was like a very difficult problem in one of her biochemistry classes. With her usual determination, she'd devoted herself to solving him.

Maybe, she told me, it hadn't been love she felt for him from the beginning. Maybe, in fact, it had been longing. Or maybe it was just her being an excellent student. That's what she'd always been: the best student in class. She'd always studied for every test, and when the test came, she'd always performed well, and perhaps that's what she was doing with her ex-boyfriend: studying him, in order to do well on the examination.

If she'd been a man, she said, maybe she'd have focused her academic energies entirely on chemistry. But she was a woman, and women are not given the option to set aside their personal lives. Women are meant to excel in school without ever sacrificing their relationships, in order to prove they can know what a man can know, while also knowing what a woman should know, a kind of knowledge that can never be set aside for a while, since, in that field, time is always ticking away.

Young women, she said, are like math and physics prodigies. They know their genius will start to fade by the time they turn thirty. As a result, they understand time in a way young men never can: how each month is gone, really gone, never to be retrieved again in this lifetime. So they can't set their lives aside in order to study. They don't have the idea that there will be time, later, to return to their lives. They have to do it all at once. They have to make all their discoveries before the age of thirty.

Or something, she said, annoyed, flicking a mosquito away, since the patio of that bar was thick with mosquitoes. Regardless, she knew from the start that her job in college was to succeed in school, and also to succeed in finding a partner, and so she had extended her brain beyond her work in the classroom to studying her ex-boyfriend.

For a moment, she stopped talking, and frowned down at her drink. She seemed to feel she was failing to explain herself clearly. Then she looked up at me. Have you read *Frankenstein*? she asked me. It's a book, among other things, about a male scientist who leaves the female world and goes to live among men. Surrounded only by men, he devotes himself wholly to science. He devotes himself so entirely to his science that he gets sick. He stops eating, stops seeing friends. He loses all sense of human morality.

It's an interesting story, she said, but have you ever wondered what would have happened if Elizabeth—his fiancée—had gone with him to study at the university? If she'd been given the opportunity? I think I know. She'd have studied so hard. She'd have had to do well to impress him, to satisfy his sense of ambition. But she'd also have loved him, and taken care of him when he worked himself to such sickness, and after he'd brought the creature to life, she'd have taken care of the creature as well. The story, she said, would have turned out completely differently.

Anyway, Anna said, the point is that when she was in college, she was not in nineteenth-century Ingolstadt, and she wasn't a man. She couldn't devote herself wholly to science. She was trying to prove herself in fields that had been traditionally dominated by men, but, at the same time, she was also trying to prove that she was still a woman. Therefore, she applied her intelligence not only to her subject but also to her ex-boyfriend. And the more she studied him, the more she felt she loved him. She worked herself, she said, into lovesickness. She had never loved to study so much. He was, she told me, her very best subject. There were times when he evaded her, as the most interesting subjects always do. From time to time, they broke up, and he left her. But he always came back. And that, she told me, was how she understood that he loved her as well: no matter what, every time they broke up, he always came back to her.

Sometimes, she told me, when they were together, she'd

start to doubt that he loved her. It was when he was with her, in other words, that she'd start to feel that he was beyond her: that she barely understood the material she'd be quizzed on. At such times, she'd be overcome with the feeling that he was getting further and further away, as though he were receding, a dot on the horizon, even when he was standing right in front of her. Then they'd break up, but he'd always come back, and, once again, she'd be full of hope. She'd feel him getting closer to her, or herself getting closer to him: a student approaching a difficult subject.

That's what happened, she said, when she got accepted to the PhD program at Austin. He told her he wanted to stay in New York. They'd broken up. Then she was in the position of Frankenstein: heading off to study alone. Though Frankenstein, of course, had the luxury of knowing that a woman was waiting for him at home. She herself had felt wretched, gut-punched, dizzyingly alone. Perhaps, given time with the sensation, she might have felt the cold thrill of freedom. But in those final days, as she was preparing to leave, she just felt abandoned. Her subject had gotten away from her.

But then, just as she was packing her boxes into her car, he simply arrived and got into the driver's seat. One minute, she'd been completely alone in the world. Then he'd gotten into the car, and her whole life had been saved. She'd been given more time to work on the problem.

He drove the whole way, she said, doing the occasional line of coke to stay up, and she slept in the back seat. The second morning on the road, she'd woken up and looked out the window to see pink lining the tangled green hills all around them. Suddenly, mysteriously, they were in Tennessee.

That, she said, was when she saw the hill full of black puppies. There must have been twenty or thirty of them, abandoned there by the side of the road, with their little pink tongues lolling out. She saw them, and she didn't tell her boyfriend to stop, and then they were gone, long gone behind them on the highway, and suddenly she was full of the most hopeless feeling. Those puppies, she realized, were gone. And, knowing that, she understood she'd never be happy.

She just wasn't, she said, a person who left. Really, at this point, if she were being honest, she'd have to admit that if she'd ever had a study, a discipline that was truly hers, it was the discipline of staying in place. It was the discipline of not running away. Of waiting patiently in one spot for the completion of an experiment.

In Austin, she said, things had changed between her and her boyfriend. For one thing, they were living together, so they stopped breaking up. For a while, for several years, she imagined that they'd settled into a new and happier domesticity. That the time frame, in other words, for understanding him had lengthened and relaxed. But then she'd learned he was cheating on her. Not once or twice, but all the time, whenever he was at a show in some other city.

She'd learned from a friend of theirs who'd assumed she already knew. But she hadn't. She'd been completely in the dark. The news came as such a shock that she'd gone to the bathroom and begun to throw up. For weeks, she'd thrown up everything she tried to eat. Why should she have suspected he was cheating on her? In the past, he'd always just left her. She'd had no idea he'd been keeping such secrets, no idea she'd overlooked such a glaring aspect of their relationship.

After that, they'd almost broken up. It had all felt like it was too much for her to handle. He was beyond her; she was prepared to admit that. She'd tried to understand him and failed. But then, at the same time, he'd been so distraught. He'd cried when she confronted him. He'd seemed like such a lost little boy: like a two-year-old who bites someone, then starts to cry when the person gets hurt. Or a dog who snaps at a child, then cowers, terrified and trembling, aware in his heart of imminent abandonment.

He'd been such a lost and pathetic little boy, she said, and she'd felt such overwhelming pity for him, and, also, such perplexity: How does a boy grow up to be such a creature?

That question—how he had become himself—haunted her all through those early nights. It was then, she said, for the first time, that she really—wholly and entirely—became a scientist in the true sense of the word. It was then that the spirit of science became the single driving force in her existence, as it did for Frankenstein when he quarantined himself in that rented attic, and saw no one, and only ventured out to raid graveyards. More than anything else, she said, she'd wanted to understand her boyfriend. She had been desperate; she had been willing to sacrifice anything in the whole world, if only she could understand how he had become such a person.

That, she told me, was when the conversations began. At night, in their bed, with the moonlight splayed over the quilt, like a pale, slender body sliced by the shades, she asked him, over and over, what he had done, and why he had done it.

He tried to explain, but he never could, or the answers kept shifting. Determined, she asked him again. She asked him the same questions, but from new angles: What had caused him to want to sleep with other women? What had it felt like at first? What had it felt like the next morning?

At some point, however, during those long and anguished conversations, she realized she wanted the kind of knowledge that doesn't come from anecdote. She wanted the kind of knowledge that can be proved: the kind that comes from physical experiment. Then she'd slept with him again.

Desperately, and visibly—to herself, at least—shaking (because, at that point, he seemed to her not only like an absolute stranger, but an absolute stranger who posed a clear and immediate threat to her), she'd slept with him. She hadn't wanted to. There was no desire left in her body, just as Frankenstein had no desire for food and sleep in the final days of his experiment. But she had wanted to watch him while he did it: to watch how he touched her, how he carried her to the bedroom. How he gazed at her tenderly, though her body was trembling, while her face—or the face of the woman he was carrying—was so frozen it seemed to be carved out of stone. Because she couldn't move it. Because she had stepped away, in order to observe him more closely.

From then on, whenever she slept with him—before his shows and after them, when he'd just come back from a trip—she kept her eyes open. She smelled his skin, to see if it smelled any different. She bit his neck, to see if it had a new texture. In other words: they resumed their old relationship, but this time she had knowledge. This time she'd bitten into the fruit. And so, from that point on, she was always gathering more. What if, for instance, she flirted with one of his friends? How, then, would he sleep with her in that bedroom with the moon cut into thin slices?

And what if, before they went home, she spent an hour in the corner talking with a girl she knew he'd recently slept with? How then would he throw her down on the bedspread? And what if she invited the young drummer into their relationship? And what if she became closer to the young drummer than he could? What if they excluded him?

Maybe what she wanted, she said, after the shock of the first discovery, was to be the one conducting the experiment. The one thing she couldn't live with was being the person experimented upon. She refused to be her boyfriend's monster. And so she became completely obsessed. She was, she told me, like Frankenstein in any one of the movies, or like any mad scientist in any movie, one of those scientists so consumed with his experiment that he stops combing his hair, and his eyes begin bulging out of his face.

As time went on, she said, she felt herself to be getting close. Everything else dropped away: her friends, her work, even her parents. But she felt herself to be approaching the end. Her results, she said, were more and more predictable. They seemed to be falling into a pattern. She'd prompt him to hurt her, and then he would. Each time, she said, she felt a little more satisfied with herself. Each time he hurt her, he was upholding her hypothesis.

At the same time, however, she felt him starting to hate her. Perhaps, she said, he had started to suspect that he was the subject of an experiment, and perhaps he wanted to es-

cape it. Perhaps he was beginning to feel his own predict-
ability.

After the drummer moved out, he'd come home one night
very drunk. Seeing him reel in through the door, Anna had
felt a strange kind of pleasure. A little thrill of fear, but one
that was controlled, because part of her experiment. She was
sitting, she said, in the living room, and she didn't get up
when she asked him—coolly, she said, just taking notes—if
he'd slept with someone else. Then, instead of answering, he
simply came over to her chair. Slowly, he approached her.
Then he leaned toward her as though he was going to kiss
her, looked at her with tenderness, and suddenly hit her.

He hit her with the back side of his hand. A strange ges-
ture: not a punch, not a slap. A weird, wide, slow arc of a
backhand. What shocked her most, in that moment, was how
she didn't hear it. The moment his hand struck her face went
silent.

Later, Anna said, when she was examining that moment
again, contemplating the silence, and also how large he had
seemed, how much bigger than a standard-sized human, she
wondered whether it had been an experiment of his own.
Whether, all night, he'd been planning it. Whether that's
why he'd needed to get drunk: because he'd been gearing
himself up to do it. Perhaps, she said, he'd wanted to see if
he could surprise her. To see if he could elicit a reaction she
hadn't controlled, the pure shock that would come over her
face if he did something she hadn't imagined.

But the thing was, she told me, she'd already imagined
it. It hadn't surprised her one bit. If she was being honest,

in addition to the pain of the impact, she'd even felt a thin thread of pleasure: to have so successfully predicted it.

After that, she said, things had become fairly extreme. Maybe they should have just ended the experiment then. But then she'd have been like Frankenstein, abandoning the monster she'd made. And, like the monster, he'd have had to follow her.

No. She'd made a horrible creature. Now she stayed and studied him. Perhaps, in this case, it was a mistake. Maybe she should have claimed to have come to the end of the experiment. Maybe, like Frankenstein, she should have acknowledged that she'd made something unnatural, and immediately abandoned him.

But the thing is, she said, a real scientist stays. There's always more you can know. There's always another end, deeper down in the tunnel. By then, she said, he was hitting her more and more. She'd stopped going out months before, but then she started having to miss work. She didn't want to go in with black eyes. Then, finally, the director of her lab threatened to fire her, and for some reason, she said, that had been that.

She'd always been a practical person. She was the one paying rent. He'd never made a dime in his life. If she lost her job, what would they do? Where else would they find the money to live? And what would become of the experiment, after all, if she couldn't pay for a place where the two of them could live together?

That, in the end, was when she'd made the decision. They'd been shut down for lack of funding. Or so she said to herself: they simply hadn't gotten the grant they needed to continue the experiment.

Then, practical person that she'd always been, she started looking for a new place to live. She didn't want to. She didn't want to walk away. To walk away now felt as though it would make the last several years a pure waste. Those years: now they'd be nothing more than the years in which she stayed in a relationship with a person who hit her. What she wanted, she said, was to turn that time into something of value. She wanted to transform those sordid years into knowledge. Losing him, losing the experiment, meant losing nearly two decades of her own life. To start over again with nothing behind her.

Or not nothing, she said. Not nothing at all. To walk away would be to start over with a monster behind her. A monster in the forest, waiting to emerge at the moment of her greatest happiness.

Still, she said, the money was gone. She knew she had to move on. Or so she said, in that bar in Austin, sitting across from me at the table under a strand of lights. Now, she said, she was just trying to stay busy. She was trying to focus on real experiments, the experiments she did at work. She kept long hours at the lab where she had a postdoc, where she was leading a project involving cutting-edge genome editing techniques. They were using bacterial enzymes to engineer mice for immunity to viruses. The enzymes could recognize and cleave to a specific sequence of DNA, then replace it with a preprogrammed mutation.

It was work, she told me, that she enjoyed. It required attention and precision. Often, she needed to stay late to feed and monitor the mice, so she didn't have to go home alone and think about whether to call her ex-boyfriend. She had to go in on the weekends, as well. And when she wasn't there, she had a colleague from the biology department who was good enough to sleep with her.

The colleague, she said, wasn't really her type. He constantly wanted to have honest discussions. He'd been in a lot of therapy. Sometimes, while they were in bed together, she'd be thinking about something else, and suddenly, from off in the distance, she'd hear him asking her if she was still there. If she was still with him.

What a question, she said. It annoyed her so much. Wasn't it enough that she'd left her body?

In those moments, she said, he was like a tiresome child in a game of hide-and-seek: like one of those younger children who couldn't handle solitude, who kept whining and trying to get you to come out without putting in any real effort, any of the effort that is the definition of the game, a game in which you try to find someone who has gone missing.

## 4.

THAT'S WHAT ANNA said. Or so I remembered, when I was sitting on the bench by the playground, watching my daughter, who had come back down the stairs and was now picking up trash once again. The memory of that conversation aggravated my nausea. It was like finding a cup of hot beer on a Saturday morning.

Such conversations had once been an important part of my life, but it had been years since I'd had one. It had, in fact, I realized, been years since I'd been really close with a friend. Once, with friends, I had spent countless hours tire-lessly inspecting the people we knew: examining our friends and loved ones in forensic detail.

Now, in the years since I'd been at work on having a fam-ily, all that close inspection had been replaced by the quiet and gentle aloneness of my life with my daughter, an alone-ness that was sometimes frightening, sometimes nothing other than wondrous: in it, I stood by night windows and watched the moon; I walked slowly through the snow with my child strapped to my chest. I had learned how nights pass; I had learned changes in the seasons that had been in-visible when I did not take long, daily walks with a child in a stroller. And I had forgotten how to live in other ways. Now, even remembering that conversation with Anna required me to brush up old habits, to recall old ways of telling stories: the little plots, scenes, and dialogue. The settings, the sprawl-ing casts of characters.

I found it exhausting. Why, I wondered, watching my daughter picking up trash, should I have to go back to that tiring way of making a story? Why should I have to remem-ber that night with Anna, a night on a dirty patio, drinking in the vague light while mosquitoes buzzed all around us? It no longer seemed as though it had any relevant place in my life, an evening from a previous existence I'd lopped off, the way you'd remove a limb that was threatening to disease the rest of your body.

And yet, that night, I'd felt very close to her. She told me that, if she had any free hours outside of work and sleeping with her colleague, she filled them by seeing me. I laughed. I told her I was glad to be of service. We ordered more drinks.

Later, I told her the story of my own failed marriage: how I hadn't known who I was; how I'd tried on a life; how, later, I'd unraveled it, and ventured off alone into a different life, a life I didn't recognize.

Yes: I'd felt very close to her. But the next time I saw her, she had regained her usual placid, unrevealing demeanor, as though nothing had ever bothered her. It felt like a slap in the face. It felt like a denial that there had ever been revelations between us. I had to wonder why I'd felt we were close. Once again, I doubted whether I even liked her.

Still, during those final months, when I was still living in Austin, we spent a lot of weekends together. Once, we even took a trip out to West Texas. She drove. I brought my dog, who sat in my lap and looked out the window. Since getting divorced, I couldn't leave him alone. Every time I left my apartment, he whined and scratched furiously at the door. I knew he missed my husband. I knew he felt as though the ties that had attached him to the world had been snipped. I knew he felt himself to be floating away, sailing off, alone, into cold blankness.

I felt that, in failing to keep my marriage together, I'd failed the dog. I'd doomed the dog to eternal uncertainty and loneliness. Therefore, I took him wherever I went, and was always soothed by having his warm, heavy shape on my lap: his chin on my leg, and the silky, knobbed shape of his head under my hand.

On the way out to West Texas, we passed strip malls and banks of white, chalky rock, then headed deeper into noth- ingness, until the highway was cutting through shoulders of pink and mauve and liver-red granite, and the bare stubbled earth stretched flat until the horizon. It was then that Anna told me she'd seen her ex-boyfriend again. She'd run into him at a show, and they'd gone home together.

"Oh," I said. "Oh, God, how do you feel?"

She shrugged and told me it wasn't bad, but it wouldn't happen again. It was, she said, an addiction. She knew she had to quit it. Sometimes you had to acknowledge that there were things you'd never know, people you'd never quite understand. But it was hard, she said, because he kept appearing. He had an uncanny ability to appear at just the wrong moment.

She was silent for a minute, focusing on the road. Then she told me it wouldn't happen again. It had just been a moment of weakness, brought on by the failure of her most recent experiment. The gene editing, she told me, hadn't quite worked. The bacterial enzyme had been programmed to replace a sequence of mouse DNA that made a protein necessary for the flu virus to latch on to. The idea had been to make mice invulnerable to the flu. But, for reasons that were still unclear, it had worked in some of the mouse embryo cells, but not all of them, and not uniformly, so some of the cells were immune and some weren't. It was called mosaicism. When they'd exposed the babies to flu, some of them got it, and some of them didn't.

So now I have a lab full of sick baby mice, Anna said, and I told her I was sorry. She shrugged. She had some ideas about what had gone wrong. She'd do it better next time. We drove a little longer in silence, until the sun started dropping over the desert, and suddenly the whole world was tinted red, as though these were the fields of some bloody battle; as though, more ambitious than the men in *Frankenstein*, who keep setting off by boat or carriage to another country, we'd left the earth behind altogether, and traveled to a bloodred planet.

# 5.

SITTING BY THE playground on the pedestrian mall in Iowa City, remembering that drive out to the desert, I felt a little bit dizzy. As though, in thinking about that trip, I'd gained speed and crossed some barrier in time, a barrier that divided my life now from all the lives I'd led before it, lives I'd led before my husband and I left New York, before Montana, before I'd ever been pregnant. Reeling a little, feeling extraordinarily nauseous, I put one hand on my belly, as though to steady myself. As though to anchor myself in the current moment.

Suddenly, behind me, I heard the whoosh of the splash pad that turned on at nine o'clock. My daughter looked up, made her mouth into an O, the universal human sign for excitement, then dropped the trash she was carrying and ran toward the water.

At the splash pad, she had always been unusually brave. Other children her age needed their parents to hold them and carry them through, or cried at the touch of the fountains, or sidled up, then screamed and ran away as soon as they came into contact with water.

But my daughter simply took a deep breath and ran in. She held her arms over her head. Each time she entered the fountain, you could see the shock of it hit her. You could see her want to scream. And yet, determined, she ran on through the full row of fountains, which towered high over her head, then crashed back, frothing. Nevertheless, she continued running. Then, clear of the fountains, she looped back around, put her arms over her head, and, once again, ran through the whole row.

Every time we went to the splash pad on the ped mall, people stopped on their way out of the market or into the hotel to marvel at my daughter. They laughed and pointed. "She's so brave," a woman with graying hair said, standing still and watching her.

She was brave. She had always been brave. It worried me, on occasion, to be the mother of such a brave daughter. What will the world do, I sometimes wondered, in the face of her courage? She was still running in and out of the fountains, and by now the initial joy and surprise had started to fade. The ecstasy of overcoming a shock had subsided, replaced, now, by a certain commitment. She seemed to be feeling the rhythm of the work she had committed to: the cold and the wet and the brightness of the sun on the water, her clothes soaked and clinging, her little Crocs pounding the pavement.

It was impossible to imagine that there had ever been a time when she didn't exist. No. There was no time when she didn't. And yet, only three years ago, in the fall of 2018, the last time I'd seen Anna, she hadn't been conceived yet. I was in Montana then, and pregnant with another baby, when Anna came to visit me. She'd brought her new boyfriend, the colleague she'd been sleeping with back when we spent time together in Austin.

He turned out to be handsome and bearded and tall. When they arrived, he had to go outside to take a call, and while Anna helped me make dinner, she told me she'd cut all ties with her ex-boyfriend. She'd realized, she said, that she wanted to have a family. Her new boyfriend seemed like he'd be a good father.

Then she asked if I wanted a beer, and I told her I was pregnant, but that it was still early, and I wasn't telling anyone yet. She looked a little bit shocked, and that's when the boyfriend came back into the house, so we dropped the subject.

I observed him through dinner. He did seem very nice. He went out of his way to make sure he never interrupted Anna when she was talking, and if he did start talking at the same time she did, he always apologized profusely. He made a point of expressing his shock about Kavanaugh's confirmation right off the bat; he made a point of expressing sympathy.

But once, at dinner, I asked him a question about work— he was in Anna's lab, but he worked on different projects— and, as he explained his projects in contrast to hers, he began to get more and more worked up about the ethical errors biochemists made in their research. He started to lecture about the socioeconomic implications of research like Anna's, and didn't let Anna get a word in edgewise, though she tried several times. Nor did he let my husband or me ask any follow-up questions, and suddenly I realized that it was a natural propensity for dominating the conversation that must have made him so sensitive about not interrupting.

We're most sensitive, I thought, about the things we're

most guilty of doing. And, meanwhile, he was going on about the need for international policies to restrict human genome experimentation, experimentation that amounted, he said, to eugenics.

He was talking specifically, he said, about the Chinese scientist who had genetically engineered those twin babies. And then he went on at great length about how there hadn't been need in that case, there had only been a desire for fame: a desire for accomplishment. The refusal to step away from a flawed experiment.

"Yes," Anna said, reaching for a slice of bread, "it's not good, but really, people wouldn't be so upset if he hadn't done such a bad job—"

But the boyfriend interrupted her. He was agitated; this was something about which he felt very strongly. "No, no," he said, "you're wrong, it doesn't matter whether he did a good job or not. Even in the very best-case scenario, you're just introducing another technology by which the rich can engineer better outcomes for themselves and their children, and the poor are left out. And that's only the beginning of things—that's not even taking into account the potential for dangerous and fatal mutations."

Then he went on at some length about other nefarious aspects of the scientist's experiment, and only later did Anna have time to explain what he was talking about: that, in recent months, a Chinese scientist, He Jiankui, had used CRISPR—those bacterial enzymes that could splice and revise DNA—to edit the gene sequence of two human embryos. They were twin girls, the offspring of HIV-positive parents. He'd intended to make them resistant to HIV. He'd engineered them, then implanted them in their mother's womb, and she'd given birth to the first two genetically engineered human babies.

But when He Jiankui revealed his results, and people began to investigate them, it turned out that the same thing had happened with his embryos that had happened to Anna's mice: only some of the babies' cells were resistant. One of them, Lulu, had enough resistant cells to avoid contracting the virus. The other, Nana, wasn't immune. Presumably she'd been tested, but at some point privacy laws had kicked in, or He Jiankui was hiding something, and no one was sure whether she'd been born HIV positive, an outcome that could have been avoided using other, available technologies.

There were, furthermore, other unintended changes as well: mutations that had yet to be studied. No one knew what sorts of health issues those altered genes would encode, whether Lulu and Nana would be vulnerable to other diseases, and whether the altered genes would be passed on through generations if Nana and Lulu survived long enough to have babies.

Also: a third baby had been discovered, who wasn't initially included in He Jiankui's reports. So somewhere, unrecorded, there was a third baby, with a third set of unprecedented mutations, who might pass those on to his children.

Altogether, there were three known babies on whom He Jiankui had experimented, and whose parents He Jiankui had misled about the risks involved in the process, and who may have gotten HIV, as well as a whole host of other unprecedented and potentially heritable maladies.

"We're all aghast, of course," Anna was saying, "and of course he did a terrible job, but I find it a little naïve to protest against the very concept of genetic engineering." First off, she said, we already do it. We're already genetically engineering the species every time we use IVF. Really, Anna said, the field of IVF is an absolute Wild West, more of a Wild West than any other field of science or technology, especially in the US, where there are fewer restrictions than any other country in the world on what you can screen for. You can choose gender, she said, or you can choose eye color. You can choose not to have a deaf or a blind baby.

I noticed that the boyfriend was opening his fourth beer, and that his nose had gotten a little bit red. But Anna was unperturbed, or she'd gotten involved enough in the topic that she didn't notice it. She was making the point that you could take the argument further, beyond IVF, to genetic testing of a fetus. What are we doing, she said, other than genetic engineering, when we allow people to have abortions because of genetic issues with the fetuses? Since we developed the capacity to test for dwarfism in utero, she said, dwarfism has declined to such a degree that we may at some point in the future live in a world with no dwarves.

What's more, she was saying, are we sure that dating apps aren't a kind of genetic engineering? When people set the program to exclude candidates of a particular height? Or when people swipe past matches of any one religion or race, or even just matches with a particular skin tone?

The boyfriend started laughing. "This is absurd," he said. "The categories you're comparing, they just aren't the same. I mean, we're talking about introducing mutations that we have no idea about. Like those rabbits engineered to be leaner who ended up having long tongues they couldn't hold inside their mouths, so they couldn't eat, or the cows engineered to have immunity to viruses who ended up resistant to antibiotics. We're talking about truly horrible possible outcomes. And you're talking about dating someone with blue eyes. You're just saying shit to say it. You don't even believe what you're saying."

Anna had finally realized he was upset, so she didn't answer, and instead shifted uncomfortably in her seat. But the boyfriend went on. He had narrowed his eyes, and was looking straight at her.

"This is what you do," he said. "You experiment for the sake of experimenting, without thinking through the effects down the line. Without thinking about the question of when it is ethically appropriate to abandon the experiment."

He wasn't talking to us anymore. Uncomfortably, Anna put down her bread. My husband started to talk about how cold it was in Montana, and it was already late, so I said I was going to bed. Exhausted as I was by my early pregnancy, I fell asleep as soon as I lay down, but later I woke up and heard Anna and her boyfriend downstairs, talking loudly. I lay awake for some time, listening to them fighting, until it started raining and the sound of the rain hitting the roof drowned out the sound of their voices.

The next morning, when I went downstairs, Anna was already up, making coffee. Wearing puffer coats, because my husband was right, it was already cold, we went out to the front porch with our mugs. The rain had brought down all the ash leaves: the black streets were plastered with pale yellow faces, and Anna apologized for the fight she'd had with her boyfriend.

She told me that she'd accidentally let him know, a few weeks earlier, that she'd still been sleeping with her ex-boyfriend when they first met. It had just slipped out. She hadn't imagined it would be a big deal. They hadn't, in those early years, ever talked about being exclusive. They just slept together once or twice a week. She explained how angry he'd been, and even though she'd apologized several times, and tried to explain that there wasn't any love left between her and her ex-boyfriend, they'd just been running an experiment on each other, he'd still been hurt. He'd insisted that she tell him the whole story: the end of her relationship with her ex-boyfriend, the way she'd continued seeing him.

I listened while she talked, but I was also paying attention to the fact that the sky had gotten grayer and lower, and that the first snow of the winter had started to fall. She'd hoped, she said, that if she told him the whole story, he'd understand. But, in fact, telling him more had made a bad situation worse. Her new boyfriend was still hurt, and still angry, but now it seemed as though he intended to punish her for her hubris in imagining she could be the one in control of the experiment.

# 6.

STANDING THERE BY the fountains of the splash pad, as the Iowa summer heat began to rise with the morning, I remembered suddenly, and with perfect clarity, how cold it had been on that porch. It was a sharp cold, a cold that made my nipples ache, since I was still pregnant with that first baby. There was a cold scent in the air. I could smell it: that hard, mineral scent, combined with the scent of wet tree bark. I could see the pale yellow leaves, clinging to the black pavement.

Suddenly, the feeling of being on that porch overwhelmed me. This had happened a few times since my daughter was born and we went into quarantine. It was as though, now that we were finally sealed off from the lives I'd lived before this point, they could revisit me with new and overwhelming brilliancy.

Never, before this time in my life, had my memories overwhelmed me like that. Now, finally, standing by the splash pad, I was overcome by the sensation of sitting there on that cold porch with Anna when I was pregnant with that first baby. But I was also aware that, in the blurred heat of summer in Iowa City, my daughter was still running through the towering fountains.

Readjusting my focus to what was in front of me was a little dizzying, and I felt, once again, the nausea sliding over me. I was so extraordinarily nauseous. Why, I wondered, had I decided to meet Anna? After that talk on the porch, we'd all gone out for a hike, and by then the trail had been snowy, and I was worried about slipping and harming the baby. That night, Anna and her new boyfriend had gone out to a bar. I'd miscarried the next morning. Or, rather, I'd gone to the doctor the next morning, and the sonogram technician had showed me my empty belly: that cloudy sky, and the baby that had been partially reabsorbed back into my body.

On the way home from the hospital, I'd called Anna and asked if she could take her boyfriend and leave a few hours early. I told her what had happened. I told her I didn't want to see anyone. She told me she'd text me when they were out, and for the next hour or so, I walked around in the snow: past the snowy playground, past the drained and snowy swimming pool.

Then Anna texted to say they were gone, and I didn't respond, and I probably should have called her at some point to apologize, but I didn't. She didn't call me, either. Probably she didn't know what to say. It wasn't until the spring, when I was pregnant again, when I finally called her, and neither one of us talked about what had happened when I rushed her and her new boyfriend out of my house.

Instead, I asked her how she was, and she told me that in the weeks after their visit, her new boyfriend had broken up with her. He hadn't been able to forgive her for what happened with her ex-boyfriend. She suspected, she said, that his feelings had less to do with how she'd still been sleeping with the ex-boyfriend, and more to do with the fact that she'd allowed him to hit her. He hadn't said as much, but she felt sure that this was the case. It had changed his opinion of her; it had diminished her. It had caused him to feel that he could more fully punish her. So he'd punished her for a while—arguing more, cutting her off, dismissing her ideas—and then he'd broken up with her.

"I'm sorry, Anna," I said. "That's awful. I'm really sorry."

"It's fine," she said, in that same flat, slightly stoned voice. "I'm glad I know what he's like. I don't want to have a baby with a person like that."

Then she told me she was looking into having a baby on her own. She was nearly forty. She wanted to do it before it was too late. For a few months after that boyfriend broke up with her, she told me, she'd tried to find another person she'd like to date, and maybe have a family with. But her desire to find someone quickly had clouded her judgment. She felt that men could smell her desperation. She had begun to suspect that they were inclined to punish it. Or maybe they just wanted to punish her for being forty and still single. For existing, as she did, outside that protected bubble of married domesticity. There was a man at a conference, she told me, at the conference hotel. Then she stopped telling the story. In the end, she said, she just didn't want to wait anymore. She knew, now, that what she wanted was to have a baby.

I looked out the window. It was April in Montana, and the field outside our house was snowy. I was nearly four months pregnant, and still extraordinarily nauseous, but at least I'd gotten through the twelve-week appointment. I was feeling hopeful, expanded, maternal. I told her I thought she should do it. I told her it was a great idea. Why should you have to wait for a man, I said, if you're ready to have a baby?

# 7.

MY DAUGHTER WAS still running. Her crocs were still pounding the pavement, her cheeks jostling in time with her movement, my little creature, this sweet girl I'd been pregnant with during those final months we spent in Montana.

I saw Anna one more time after that conversation by the

window, when I looked out at that snowy field and told her I thought she should have a baby alone. It was in August. I was seven months pregnant and giving a reading in Austin. Anna picked me up at the airport. In the car, we talked about how drastically the Austin airport had changed in the few years since I'd lived there. It almost felt, I said to Anna, as though I were arriving in a brand-new city: a glass and metal city, a city built from scratch on a new planet.

The sun was setting over the enormous car lots that lined the highway, the Party Barns, the strip clubs, and the arterial exits. The sky was magnificent: tangerine laced with fluorescent pink. But when I commented on how pretty it was, Anna shrugged: sunsets like that, she said, were the result of pollution from the El Dorado fires.

I asked whether those were the fires that had been caused by the gender reveal. She nodded. "As everyone is eager to comment upon," she said. "As though, in fact, those fires weren't caused by global warming. As though the real crime were a party some people find tasteless."

I recalled what I'd read about that fatal gender reveal: the rocket, with smoke that was either blue or pink, that had exploded and set off the most recent worst fires in California history. I wondered how far along the woman was now. I wondered whether it was a girl or a boy. Anna, meanwhile, turned off the highway at South First. We had reservations for dinner at a Vietnamese restaurant I'd liked when I lived there, and though it was a few years old, it was as glassy and new as the airport.

It was, in fact, like an outpost of the airport, but with rickety vintage chairs painted white, and misters over the patio. We took a metal filigree table. Anna had a cocktail; I had a shrub. We sat under the misters. Back in Montana, it still occasionally snowed; here, between the humidity and the misters, I was slowly getting wet while Anna told me she'd begun the process of getting pregnant. She'd bought vials of sperm from the Sperm Bank of California. They'd been delivered to the clinic. She'd tried three rounds of IUI, horrified and amazed, each time, by how janky and unscientific the whole process was. She'd arrive at the clinic and they'd give her the unfrozen vial, instructing her to hold it with both hands to keep the sperm dark and warm. Then they'd send her to the waiting room. There she would sit, in the bright, coldly air-conditioned room, clutching her vial with both hands, aware of the millions of potential lives she was holding.

Often, they'd keep her waiting for half an hour, clutching her vial, and when she finally got into the room where the procedure would take place, they'd tell her to undress, and she'd feel like crying: How could she do that, while clutching her vial? Finally, one of the nurses gave her the tip that many women tucked the vial into their bra. So she learned to tuck the vial into her bra to keep it warm and dark while she undressed from the waist down. Then she'd sit on the examining chair, and fit her feet into the cold stirrups, and finally deliver the vial to the nurse, who, with horrifying casualness, would set it down on the counter, the cold counter under the glaring white lights. With her feet in the stirrups, she'd watch that little vial, her heart beginning to palpitate, wondering how many of the sperm were dying.

Anyway, it hadn't worked, so she'd switched to IVF. It

had been a hard couple of months, she said. They pump you full of so many hormones. First, they put you on birth control. Then they get you off. Then they start the more serious hormones. Every night, because she had no partner to help her, she'd had to inject herself with the shots. Alone, in her apartment, preparing her syringe, getting ready to shoot herself full of hormones, she'd felt insane. As though she were a mad scientist, experimenting on her own body.

Then she'd observed all the effects of the treatment: the nausea, the hot flashes at night, and the headaches. And she'd been so emotional—one minute hopeless, the next overjoyed, the next with a heart full of bloody murder: to be a body experimented upon in the unregulated field of fertility treatment. She'd hated everything her doctors said. She'd felt like their monster: out of control of her own body. It had filled her with rage, which made her doubt her capacity to be a good mother.

But she'd also been excited. At night, she'd had the most incredible dreams. The hormones, it seemed, had unlocked a vast and previously unexplored realm of her subconscious. Every night, she dreamed of having a baby. In recent months, she'd had so many dream children. As a result, it had been a shocking disappointment when none of the embryos had worked out. They'd told her the afternoon after the harvesting procedure. She was still foggy with anesthetic, and so, despite her training, which had often involved the creation of embryos, and the fact that, sometimes, even when all the right ingredients are combined in the petri dish, an embryo just doesn't take, she felt she didn't understand what they meant. She made them explain it to her, step by failed step.

Still, she couldn't quite comprehend it. She realized she hadn't even considered the possibility that this might be the outcome: that not one of the eleven eggs they'd harvested that month would become a successful embryo.

They'd told her, she said, up front, that they would rate the embryos. That they'd give them scores of excellent, good, fair, and poor. And that they didn't recommend implanting fair and poor embryos. That, though in very rare cases they'd seen a fair or poor embryo develop into a live birth, most often they became a miscarriage.

She'd been prepared, she said, to make that decision, though when they first introduced it, it had struck her as brutal. But she had not been prepared for the fact that not one of the eleven eggs would become an embryo. And so, once again, she'd readied herself to harvest more eggs. Once more, she'd spent her evenings gathering the flesh of her belly and preparing to inject it with hormones. Her whole torso was covered in bruises; if anyone had seen, they'd have thought she was in the most horrifically abusive relationship. But that wasn't the worst of it. The worst of it was her fear that it wouldn't work out. They'd done another ultrasound after her last failed month. Her egg reserve, she said, had significantly dropped. It had become low. These eggs, the eggs she was coaxing out with those hormones, should be considered—the doctors had told her—the last of her available options. Therefore, when she was giving herself those shots, she knew she was setting up her final experiment. She'd spent the month in a state of anxiety, telling herself not to feel anxious, because anxiety decreased the chances of getting pregnant.

Then, once again, she'd gone under. And her doctors had

harvested the eggs she'd produced. And now, she told me, she had to confront the fact that she was empty. There were no more good eggs in her ovaries. "In my mind," she said, "I keep wondering, 'What's a woman without any eggs?' It's like the setup for a sexist joke, but I don't know what the punch line is."

Old, I thought. A woman without any eggs has become old. But I didn't say that. The cruelty of the thought had startled me, a thought that seemed to have been implanted in my brain without my permission, and so, pregnant, safe on the other side of my own sense of humor, I scrambled to say something less hurtful. "At least now you don't have to worry about getting pregnant accidentally," I said, laughing a little at my own joke, except that Anna's right cheek was suddenly flushed.

"Oh, Anna," I said, getting hot. "I'm sorry. It was a stupid joke. I didn't think."

For a moment, she looked down at her drink. It was red: something involving beet juice. Then she shrugged. "It's okay," she said. "It's true. I've thought about it, too."

"Do you know yet?" I asked, changing the subject. "Did they already make the embryos?"

They had, she told me. This time it had worked. They'd managed to create seven embryos, four of them excellent or good. Now she was waiting on the results of the genetic screening, something she'd decided to do in advance. It was not, she said, an easy decision. She was aware of the moral implications of screening embryos for preferable traits.

But then, of course, so much of the process so far hadn't been natural. And, furthermore, she had to wonder: What, after all, in these end times we lived in, was still really "natural" at all? Every time, she said, that she went to the grocery store she saw extra-large eggs from genetically engineered birds; she saw lemons the size of small footballs. Even the sunsets, our sublime sunsets: they were just the results of smoke from unnatural forest fires.

That's what she'd realized, when she was debating whether to screen her embryos: that she didn't want to make her decision based on some sort of sentimental, nostalgic sense of what was "natural." What was natural was death in childbirth. What was natural was high infant mortality. Maybe she didn't want to screen for eye color or gender, but if she could screen for those conditions that would increase the chances of miscarriage or stillbirth, why wouldn't she want to do that? She only had seven chances. How devastating would it be, then, if one or more of them were miscarried?

Even that decision was complicated, however, by the fact that screening embryos can cause damage, or, as one of the doctors said to her, will inevitably cause a very small but not entirely insignificant amount of damage to the embryo. Could she, she wondered, justify harming her embryos just to avoid the pain of having a miscarriage down the line, especially since even screening them didn't guarantee against an aneuploidy, since there was no way to screen for full sets of extra chromosomes?

And yet: the numbers showed that screening the embryos increased your chances of live birth. And so she'd decided, and she'd also decided not to have them implant the fair or poor embryos, embryos that couldn't even get tested because the stress of the test would probably destroy them, but instead to wait for the good and excellent ones to come back from testing. And, at first, she felt guilty, but then she thought: I am not choosing against the poor and fair embryos, I'm only doing everything in my power to allow the strongest one of these seven extraordinarily vulnerable little creatures to flourish. And why, she was saying, shouldn't she do whatever she could to protect and nourish her child, just as she would after the child was born?

She continued to describe the long debate she'd had with herself, before deciding to send her embryos away to be tested, but I wasn't listening anymore. I'd stopped listening back when she was talking about how devastating it would be if she were to miscarry one of her seven embryos, and how she felt it was her duty to protect her embryos from such a fate, and suddenly I realized that the last time I'd talked with Anna in person, I'd still been pregnant with my first baby.

It had been so cold on that porch. Now, in Austin, it was hot, and the misters were pumping. When I looked at myself in the window, I realized that my eye shadow had smudged, as though I'd spent the whole dinner crying. I was seven months pregnant. My face was puffy. In the glass, I was nearly unrecognizable to myself.

I ordered another shrub. Anna ordered another cocktail. She was tipsy by the time we got the check, so I drove her car back to the hotel.

There, we changed into bathing suits and went to the pool. It was an enormous, glowing kidney set just off the street, surrounded by the sounds of people coming in and out of nearby bars. We were across from the bar where we used to go see Anna's ex-boyfriend play shows with his band. Lights on the arrow pointing into its door turned the water yellow, then red, and Anna was working on the complimentary bottle of wine that we'd found in the hotel room.

It was strange, to be back in that place. To be back there with Anna. I couldn't decide whether I felt as though that whole time in my life seemed impossibly distant, or whether it seemed impossibly close. For a moment, I realized that a major difference between Anna and myself was that I'd left the place where my life had fallen apart. I'd left, and started a new life in a new city. Anna, on the other hand, still drank wine on the same street where we'd once gone to her ex-boyfriend's shows.

I kicked my feet in the glowing red pool, and she started to tell me about how strange it was to find sperm on the sperm bank website. She'd spent months, she said, perusing donor profiles. There were descriptions of their hobbies, test scores, education degrees. They couldn't include photographs, because they had to protect the donors' anonymity, but there were baby pictures, or photographs from school picture day. "It feels," she said, "like you're on a dating website for pedophiles."

I started laughing. She laughed, too, a second late, as though surprised to learn that the idea was humorous. Then she spilled some red wine on the pavement and started laughing even harder, then asked if I wanted to see her donor. We dried off and went inside; I got out my laptop and she pulled him up. There he was: a serious-looking boy with dark, curly hair and dark eyes. It was a school photo, with one of those marbled blue backgrounds. He was wearing a cable-knit sweater vest.

"Oh, Anna," I said. "He's adorable. You're gonna have an adorable baby."

Anna smiled. She gazed at him fondly. "He is cute," she said, "isn't he?"

Then she started to show me her other favorite donors. In addition to the childhood photographs, there were lists of various attributes: eye color, height, skin tone. We opened the paragraphs the donors had written, paragraphs that read like bad college essays, describing the donors' ambitions and interests: how they loved skydiving and spelunking, or had always known they wanted to study medicine.

For a moment, I felt like a twenty-one-year-old, looking online to find a boyfriend. Helpfully, the personal essays were accompanied by descriptions written by workers at the sperm bank: this donor held the door for the nurses; this donor was always on time for his appointments; this donor made jokes with the receptionist. This donor looked like Chris Pratt; this donor looked like a young Eddie Murphy. Perusing these options in my hotel room in Austin, Anna and I were giddy. She was nearly finished with the free bottle of wine—she'd told me she was going to drink because it was a special occasion, and she was in the month of waiting to receive the results of the genetic testing—and we were both laughing too loud. We were laughing as though we were making prank phone calls, or as though we were venturing onto a dating website for the first time, but without any of the anxiety that comes with dating when you're nearly forty.

It was as though we had been given the option to start over again, to start over as girls, but with all the knowledge we'd gained from living to middle age. This time, Anna wouldn't waste her youth on her ex-boyfriend. This time, instead of creating a monster, she intended to make a baby, a baby she'd stay to take care of, with all the tenderness that Frankenstein denied his own unfortunate creature. We'd been given a second chance, a chance to live a gentler story. All these men, no more than boys, smiling on school picture day: they seemed so perfectly unthreatening. Smaller than average, rather than larger, and with symmetrical little faces, unlined by experience. They seemed to be the exact opposite of monstrous, and, anyway, we'd never met them. We never would. It was like a dating website, but there would be no date: not one that could go wrong in a small but still saddening way, nor in a more frightening manner. There would be no date that might go well, but later develop into something incorrect, wasting precious time you'd never regain in real life.

These young men wasted none of your time. They made jokes; they held the door. Obediently, they delivered their sperm into cups. None of the sperm bank employees ever said, This one seems like he might be a brute, or This one might be violent. All the traits listed were good ones, or traits that could be good for someone. It was, basically, an enormous online cafeteria of excellent genetic traits, so, giddily, we perused the details of each donor, until we realized it was late, and, anyway, Anna already had all the sperm that she needed. She'd used it to make embryos. Seven embryos. Each one of them a potential baby.

# 8.

THAT NIGHT, ANNA slept on the couch. In the morning, she drove up to the university to teach, and I had the day to myself before giving my talk. I walked up South Congress, and saw, in the light of day, how much the city had changed since I'd left. Heading north, I could see that the cranes—an ever-present part of the downtown skyline during the years when I'd lived in Austin—were now gone. The sky-rises were finished. On both sides of the street, what had once been quirky boutiques and secondhand shops had been replaced by fancy restaurants.

Once I'd crossed the bridge, where, in the evening, people had always gathered to see an exodus of bats, I began to head up the trail that followed Shoal Creek. It was still early, but the air was already humid and hot. Slightly dazed, I kept stopping to look around at the world that had, overnight, so drastically changed: cold, white, and green in Montana; hot and brown here in Austin. The live oaks along the creek were slung with Spanish moss; birds were cawing like rusty gates swinging open.

Unlike South Congress, this part of town still bore a resemblance to the place it had been when I'd lived here. The farther north I headed, the more unchanged it was. I began to feel the creeping realization that I wasn't in some newly conceptualized city, a city built from scratch, but the same place I'd lived for years: the city where I was married before. The city where I'd unraveled my marriage, where my life had gone from solid to liquid, and everything seemed to be floating away.

There was a time when it had seemed to me that I wouldn't survive it. Then I'd moved to New York, and met my second husband, and a life had solidified around me again. But even so, for a few years, it had been too difficult to return to this city. Each time I landed, and walked out of the airport into the humid air, I'd felt my heart begin to beat wildly.

Even years later, remarried and pregnant, I felt my throat begin to constrict as I headed up the trail along Shoal Creek and thought about those awful months after my divorce, when I'd searched for a place I could afford on my own, and signed a lease, and lived in the state of siege that settled over and around that wretched apartment.

As it had been when I lived in that apartment, the creek that ran along the path was low because of drought. The grass on the other side of the path was as brown as it had been during those difficult months, when the legislature had passed the first Texas law making most abortions illegal, as well as the law allowing the open carry of handguns; as brown as it had been when I lived in that apartment that looked out on the alley full of trash cans and agave, where my landlord paced, his shoulders hunched and his fists clenched, and sometimes stopped to peer in through the windows.

What a strange way to live, I thought now, seven months pregnant and walking alone along that dried creek. How had things come to such a bad state? When I'd first visited that apartment, I'd felt some apprehension about signing the lease. After the showing, the landlord asked me to come to his house to have a cup of green tea. His house was next door, a large, visibly decaying Victorian. When we stepped in the front door, he apologized for the clutter that made it difficult to walk down the hallway. He reached out to help me step over a box. Once we had made our way through the clutter, into an office, the door of which was now blocked by piles of old newspapers, he explained to me in a soft, concerned tone of voice that, having had several regrettable experiences with his tenants, he was looking to rent to "the right kind of person." He wondered, he said, with a gentle and strained little laugh, whether I was such a candidate.

After that meeting, I'd been concerned. But it was a good neighborhood and a good price, and it had become hard for me to find apartments I could afford in that city, so I signed the lease and moved in, only to find that one of the street-facing windows was missing. It was a rectangular hole, surrounded by wood. I stood in front of it, confused, startled by how empty it looked.

When I called him, my landlord—in the same gentle but strained tone of voice—explained that, in the days leading up to the move, he'd been attempting to repair one of the frames and had accidentally broken the pane. He reassured me that he'd have it covered by the end of the day, and that he'd replace the glass pane by the end of the weekend.


LATER THAT DAY, I laughed about the window with Anna. She'd come over to help me unpack. When she expressed concern about my empty window, I told her about the landlord's cluttered house. "He's strange," I said, "but nothing to worry about." She opened the wine she'd brought, and the plastic clamshell containers of salad, and we laughed together about my predicament, newly divorced, moving into an apartment without any glass in the windows. We'd just finished assembling the IKEA couch. Now we were opening boxes of books, unloading them into stacks under the window.

My boxes had been in storage since I got divorced, when I moved hastily out of the house I shared with my husband. It was a nice feeling to be unpacking those books, a little reunion of sorts, or it was a nice feeling until I opened the last box and suddenly the room was overwhelmed with the most hideous stench. It was a sickly sweet scent. Something had died in that box. Fearfully, I pulled out book after book. They all smelled equally bad until I found my copy of *The Portrait of a Lady*. There was a hole in the cover. A mouse had burrowed in through Isabel Archer's face, shredding a nice little nest, where it must have urinated profusely, yellowing and warping the pages, until at some point it suffocated to death.

Anna started to gag. I got out a rag and cleaning solution, but none of the books were salvageable. We ended up taking the whole box out to the dumpster behind the coffee shop, and by nightfall, after Anna had gone home, my landlord had, indeed, covered the empty frame with clear plastic sheeting.

But even by the end of the weekend, he hadn't replaced the glass pane. By then, I was beginning to grow somewhat concerned. I thought about calling my ex-husband. But he, I knew, would have reassured me that all was well, that there was nothing to worry about. Unsure what to do instead, I sat for some time on the couch and looked out the window of my new apartment, the one that wasn't covered in plastic.

It faced the alley. Along it, the trash cans and the enormous agaves were illuminated by cones of light from the streetlamps. A cat slunk between the trash cans, his eyes glowing like a raccoon's. I sat very still. The window was open. It was very hot, well over a hundred degrees, and I could hear the neighbor's pet goat, her bell tinkling when she jumped up onto the roof of the shed. I didn't think to turn on any lights. I just sat there, looking out the window, listening to the goat's bell and the rustling of the plastic sheeting.

Over the subsequent weeks, I often sat on the couch, looking out the intact windows that faced onto the alley, and saw my landlord striding up and down in front of the trash cans, wearing cargo shorts and athletic socks pulled up to his knees, peering anxiously in through the glass. He never made any effort to fix the window that still had no pane.

At some point, I realized that the lock on my front door was also broken. When I asked my landlord to fix it, he told me, wearily, as though he had finally come to the end of his rope, that the broken lock was in fact symptomatic of a much larger problem, a problem with the shape of the door frame. While he would do his best to address it, he said, there were also other repairs on his list. He needed, he told me, to fix two more of my windows.

Then he reminded me that he'd asked me to buy a rug to place over the carpeting in the bedroom, in order to prevent wear and tear. He'd seen, he said, that I hadn't, and he would appreciate it if I'd rectify that.

The following afternoon, when I came home from teaching, two more of my windowpanes had been removed. There was plastic over the panes. I sat down on the couch. I could hear the plastic rustling.

ALL THAT FALL, while the Halloween decorations danced on my neighbors' porches and I longed for the former certainties of my life, or the aspects of my life that I had once imagined were certain, I felt extraordinarily uneasy. With no real reason that I could point to, I felt as though I was living under a threat. Perhaps it was the lock on the front door that was still broken. Or perhaps it was those open windows, or the new laws, which had caused all the Planned Parenthoods to close down and the university to hold seminars on how to behave if one of your students was openly carrying a handgun. Or perhaps it was the presidential election that was still somewhat distant, though the debates between candidates for the Republican nomination had been marked by increasingly alarming rhetoric.

But, if I'm honest, all that seemed far away. And, in fact, even the missing windows and the unlocked door were threats I'd grown accustomed to, so when I lay awake through the night, I couldn't really be sure what it was I was so worried about. And yet I was, and it was difficult for me to focus, and in November I started to think that I needed to move to a new city.

It was time, I said to myself, for me to start over. I couldn't start over on those old foundations.

But, at the same time, I didn't know where to go. My whole adult life, this had been my home. And so I moved through my days, caught in one place as though in a spell, listening to the warm wind rustling in the plastic sheeting over my windows, as though I had moved from a home to ship, and those were the sails, flapping above me.

Then, suddenly, though it had remained oddly hot through the fall, it became cold. In the mornings, when I took the dog out for his walk, each blade of grass was covered with frost. To protect them from the cold, people had draped white sheets over the cacti in their yards, so that, though Halloween had already passed, it seemed as if they'd decorated their houses with ghosts.

Inside, I turned the heat on, but that apartment never got warm, perhaps because of the plastic over the windows, so I kept turning the heat up and up until one day, when I came home from teaching, I wrote my landlord and told him I needed to leave. To make the email easier, to make myself seem more responsible and put-together, I lied. I said I'd gotten a job in a new city. I told him that, in accordance with policies listed on the tenants' rights website, I'd given him three months' notice. I was aware that I'd lose my deposit.

Two days later, he replied to my email. He let me know, in no uncertain terms, that he could not permit me to leave the apartment. He felt, he told me, betrayed by the suggestion. While he was sure that I did not intend to harm him by writing my email, I had, nevertheless. His health, he told me, had deteriorated that fall, and he was awaiting medical procedures. "Whatever illusions I may have had," he said, "about being in control of my work and stress in the new year have been summarily taken away from me."

He went on to say that while he understood his obligations under the law, he could not permit me to get out of my lease. He suggested that we meet with a conflict-negotiation specialist.

I refused. It was clear to me that I needed to leave. I'd heard the sails rustling; I'd heard the call of the sea. The next day I delivered him written notice of my intent to vacate. He posted a sign to my door, stating that he didn't accept it. I began to make preparations to move. The next day he posted a new sign to my door, and the next day another, notifying me of my various failures. He had researched my background; he had facts to share about my upbringing, my education. Then he built a wooden hutch outside the window over my desk—now covered with plastic—and began to come every day to work on the frame, sitting on an overturned bucket, using an electric drill to make holes.

So January passed, and February, new notes posted daily, construction continuing on the windows, tensions rising in and around that little apartment, and finally we came to the week before the date on which I'd stated that it was my intention to leave.

Then I started packing my things. Hourly, now, he strode down the alley and glared in the windows, his fists clenched and his shoulders hanging down from his ears. Nevertheless, I packed, in more and more of a frenzy, becoming more anxious to get out with each lap he took up the alley, so that eventually, to speed up the process of packing, I began driving carloads of possessions—books I no longer liked, clothes that once fit me, an odd wedding dress—to the dumpster behind the coffee shop.

It was as I was preparing to carry the final box out to my car that I heard a forceful knock on the door with no lock.

My stomach dropped, expecting my landlord, but it was, instead, a nervous little man wearing a tan polo shirt, no badge, and a large gun in a holster displayed so prominently on the front of his belt that it was, in fact, something of a relief when he merely delivered the notice of my landlord's intent to sue me.

WALKING ALONG SHOAL Creek toward the intersection where I climbed up away from the water, passed a bank of chalky rock, then crossed Lamar and headed into the neighborhood where I used to live, I remembered that moment: standing in my doorway, looking down at that little man with his gun strapped to the front of his belt.

How strange it was, seven months pregnant, with a whole new life in a new part of the country, to be coming back to that neighborhood where once I'd lived with such a sense of looming threat: as though I were living my life in the shadow of an iceberg approaching my ship. I had escaped; I had returned to safety. But still it was strange to come back.

I was safe, of course, back then as well. Or so I thought, heading up the steep hill next to the bike shop. In the end, after my landlord sued me, I'd moved in with Anna. A friend of hers from college, an entertainment lawyer, had helped me draft a countersuit, listing all the illegal aspects of the rental: the missing windows, the broken lock, the harassing notes on the door. After a few weeks, when my landlord didn't respond to the countersuit with a court date, I simply moved to New York, and hoped my landlord didn't take me to court, which would have required me to fly back and hire a lawyer.

I had, in other words, all the resources I needed to be safe: friends with extra rooms, other friends who were lawyers. I'd received the final payment for the book I'd recently published. I had plenty of money to lose my deposit and also move to New York. Or so I thought, walking along the streets of that quiet, safe neighborhood: the pecan trees, casting their tumbling shadows over the street; the student housing; the quiet sidewalks; the nice houses with Tibetan Buddhist pennants hung over their porches; the cheese store and the yoga studio and the French café. Really, I thought, was it so much of a problem not to have locks? Was it so much of a problem not to have windows, if at any point I could have left?

It had been so easy, in the end, to simply move in with Anna. The first night, we'd both gone to sleep early. The second night, she'd asked me if I wanted to go out to a show. But I was still tired after the last weeks in that apartment, so I stayed home and watched TV. When she came home, she barely said hello to me. She went to the bathroom and took a long shower, and then she went into her bedroom. I could smell weed through the crack under the door.

An odd way of coming home to a visiting friend. That, perhaps, was the only burden involved with living with Anna: her odd coldness, her scientific remove, the fact that, so often, she went into her bedroom to smoke weed alone. Through the next several weeks, while I stayed in her extra bedroom and drafted my countersuit, she went to work and came home and was basically polite, but every night she went into her bedroom and smoked weed until she went to sleep.

It was a little bit startling how unfriendly she was, given the fact that she'd invited me to come stay. But I assumed she was a person who liked her own space, and I was grateful that she was letting me have her spare bedroom, so I didn't make an issue of it when two or three weeks passed in that manner, until finally, on the last night, when I was preparing to leave for New York, she came into my room and asked me if I could do her a favor.

She needed me to stay an extra night. She needed me to come with her, she said, when she got an ultrasound.

Then, in that same flat and placid tone of voice, she told me she'd slept with her ex-boyfriend again. She'd seen him at a show; she'd been drunk and she'd flirted with him. Then he'd walked her to the car, and in an alley he'd pushed her up against the wall and had sex with her.

It wasn't good, she said. She was asking him not to, and crying, and telling him she'd gone off the pill. But he did it anyway, and she didn't fight him off. It seemed simpler, she said, to give in.

Afterward, because she was shaking too much to drive, and her forehead was bleeding from where it had been pressed against brick, he sat with her on the curb and told her he loved her. He stayed with her until she stopped shaking. Then she got into her car and drove home.

The next morning, before work, she went to Planned Parenthood to get the morning-after pill, and to make an appointment for STD testing, but the Planned Parenthood where she used to go had shut down. She stood there on the sidewalk for a while, uncertain where else she should go, but then she realized how late she was for work, so she decided to forget it. What were the chances? She put it in the back of her mind. She focused on her work in the lab.

And then she must have lost track of time. She had no idea when her last period was, but this one seemed late, so she took a pregnancy test. For a moment, she considered keeping the baby, but that would have been it: her ex would have been in her life forever, the two of them torturing each other, using everyone around as collateral, and what kind of life, she said, would that be for a baby?

Not a good one, she thought, not even a safe one. She could not, she told herself, bring a new life into such a violent environment. It would have been, she said, like Frankenstein making a bride for the monster he'd made, or like Frankenstein allowing the monster to have children, even after he'd proven that he could be a murderer. No, she said, she would not: she had to gather up the last remaining pieces of that awful experiment and throw them into the water.

Then she made an appointment at a new clinic to get mifepristone, and they let her know it was now a requirement that she should get an ultrasound. And she'd been planning to go alone, but she wondered if I would be willing to come.

AT THE DOCTOR'S office, we parked in the covered lot, and while we walked through the concrete, echoing space, I remembered that my mother always warned me to never park in covered lots because once, when she was young, she'd been attacked in one. She was getting into the elevator. A man helped her with the door, let it close, then pulled a knife out of his jacket.

I reached for Anna's hand. I was expecting her to swat it away, but without changing her expression, she took it, and held it, and kept my hand in hers while we took the elevator up. She kept it while she was checking in, and while we waited in the waiting room surrounded by all those rounded, happier women. She kept it even when the nurse came out and called her name, and I began to walk with her toward the door, but the nurse looked at her clipboard, frowned, then told me only her husband could come with her.

Then I sat down again. I read a *Sunset* magazine while I waited, and when Anna came out, her face was stony.

"Are you okay?" I asked her, while we were walking out to the car.

"Fine," she said. "I had a nice technician. I've never been penetrated so gently."

That night, we watched *The Bachelor* and drank wine. The mifepristone hadn't kicked in yet, or hadn't yet kicked in in earnest; she was just taking Advil for some mild cramping. I asked her if she wanted me to stay with her when the bleeding started. She thanked me, but told me she wanted to be alone. This was her mess, she said, to clean up. And so the next morning I left, and drove to New York, and started a new life in a new city, but really, even now, this neighborhood where I once lived when my life was coming apart still made me feel extremely uneasy. I couldn't stand it. Even now, all these years later, so I turned back and headed down to the creek and walked along it until I got to Town Lake. That night, I gave my reading, and afterward, as soon as I could get away, I took a cab to the airport, and I'd just gotten through security when I got a text about my flight being delayed.

They would text me, they said, when they had an update. I went to the gate. Everyone was standing around, waiting for the update. I felt myself getting nervous. What if the flight were delayed a long time? What if I had to stay another night in that city? The airport was new and glassy, but it still smelled like barbecue. Everywhere I looked, outlined in neon, were the severed heads of longhorn cattle. I kept waiting to see someone I knew, someone from the life I led in that city.

Once, I had loved it. Then it became a difficult place for me to live. I'd left, and I'd tried not to come back. It had been too hard to accept the good along with the bad. I'd had to steel myself completely against it. If I were a braver person, perhaps, I wouldn't have had to operate like that. I could have looked them both in the face: the good, and also the bad. But I wasn't that brave. I disliked the city. I didn't want to think about it. Certainly, I didn't want to stay another night.

And perhaps it was my relief when we finally started boarding, my relief about leaving Texas, about leaving that difficult time I'd concluded absolutely and somewhat artificially, as Walton abandons his life in England, and sets out for the unknown expanse of the Arctic, that made me ignore my phone when Anna called me that fall.

But also, I was busy. My husband and I had left Montana and moved to Iowa, and there was a house to furnish, and new classes to teach, and then I gave birth to a baby who seemed to have been sent from the moon, and nearly bled out, and came home to a new planet, a place farther and more remote than the Arctic, as though I'd sailed up to the North Pole and kept sailing, a lunar distance from Earth, where everything that had happened before, including my friendship with Anna, seemed so impossibly distant that I didn't feel guilty when I ignored another phone call that winter.

And then the pandemic arrived, and we went into quarantine, and our baby was home with us while we were working full-time, so, truly, I was very busy. And, really, I didn't feel guilty. Or so I said to myself: that I didn't feel guilty, not when I didn't call her that winter, or that summer, or even the following winter.

That year and a half when I didn't call Anna: what a warm time it was in my life. Of course, somewhere else, everything was falling apart. But the whole time, we were together: my husband and my daughter and me. We had sailed off to the moon. All those months, we barely ever left the house. Our groceries were delivered. First it was winter, and we lit fires together in a pit we made in the backyard. Then it was spring, and the daffodils and the cherry blossoms came out. The days lengthened. Far away, there were murder and disease and rising tide lines, but in our backyard, our daughter was crawling.

At the end of the summer, a derecho, an unprecedented weather event, swept through Iowa City, knocking down half the trees on our street. It took out power for over a week, but we were safe in the basement, me and my husband and our little baby, and when we emerged to find that the enormous pine tree by our driveway had fallen over our car, we could only laugh. How strange it was, on those clear days that followed the storm, to walk with our baby around our altered neighborhood. It seemed that half the trees were now gone, leaving gaping absences.

That fall: it passed as though it were filmed during the most luminous hour of the day, with light streaming in through the windows, surrounding our baby with gold. She had started to walk. We planted two pear trees. When the leaves fell, she grew four little teeth. That winter, she played in the snow. By the time I finally listened to the voice mails Anna had left me, I was trying, once again, to get pregnant. And so, for the third time in three years, I was tracking my ovulation and waiting to see if I missed my period, a strange kind of suspension of normal time that I had come to know well: a way of life that doesn't mark time chronologically, not by the sun, not by the passing days, but by the moon, and according to the ebbs and tides inside my own body.

It was winter, and there had been snow on the ground for over a month, snow heaped on the branches of the remaining trees, so that the sky was white and gray, and the ground was white and gray also, and the trees seemed to be wearing white dresses. I was walking with my baby strapped to my chest. Together, we surveyed the snowy emptiness, my baby and I, alone, only the two of us on this planet, and for some reason, from that echoing distance, I remembered Anna trying to have a baby alone, something I had encouraged her to do, before promptly abandoning her.

That was when I felt a pang of guilt. When I checked my phone to see when she'd called me last, I realized that she'd left me two voice mails. I hadn't noticed; it was so rare that I ever looked at my voice mail. But there was a message from Anna from over a year ago.

I pressed play, and there was her voice in my ear, telling me that she'd tested her excellent and good embryos, and only one of them was viable. The next message, left in the fall, didn't address the fact that I hadn't called her back the last time. She was letting me know she'd had a miscarriage. Ten days after the embryo had been transferred, she'd had a positive pregnancy test. But two days later, the doctors had let her know that her HCG levels were falling, and that, most likely, the embryo hadn't implanted properly. It would bleed out, they told her, with her period.

I put my phone away. I felt bad that I hadn't called her. I really did; I felt awful. But now it had been so long since she left that message. She'd probably written me off. Who knew whether she'd still want to hear from me? And if I did call her, what would I say? I seemed not to know anymore what friends said to each other. The world of people I'd once been close to had receded so far. It felt impossible to simply dial her number.

Still, I did keep thinking about her. I thought about her the rest of that day, and also that night, when my daughter was sleeping. I wondered why I hadn't called her. Somehow, at some point, other people had become difficult for me to have in my life. Their sorrows, and their happiness: at some point it had all begun weighing too much. Or perhaps it had simply seemed too far away: as though the sorrow and the happiness of my friends had become akin to the sorrow and the happiness that one reads about in the newspaper, sorrow and happiness that belong to unknown people who live in unknown countries. Perhaps I could have imagined it, but it would have been difficult. How can one go on with one's life, trying to imagine all the world's sorrow?

But how, I wondered, had I come to such an extreme

point: that even people I knew—even my friends—had become too difficult? Recognizing that, I felt ashamed. I wished I could have been there for Anna. I thought about how, when I'd miscarried, I'd felt as though I'd left the planet. And I'd been lucky. Some women have miscarriage after miscarriage. Anna had tried everything to get pregnant. Her path to becoming pregnant had been so much harder than mine. And then she'd miscarried her baby.

So I thought about her all that night, and all the next day, and even though I didn't call her, I thought of her often throughout those months when we were trying and failing to get pregnant, and later when I was pregnant, and began to feel extraordinarily nauseous again.

By then, however, I thought of her less. I was spending all my energy just getting through the day; I'd stopped thinking about Anna, or, really, anyone else, and so I was surprised when she called me again. "Strangely," she said, "I just moved to Iowa City." And she said she had news. She would explain more when she saw me.

# 9.

AND SO THERE I was, watching my daughter running in the splash pad—her initial joy having transitioned to something quieter and more focused: an attention to work, the determination to complete it—when I saw Anna walking down the ped mall, this friend from another time in my life. After more than two years, she looked the same. She was wearing jeans and a T-shirt, her hair pulled back in a ponytail, her face still somewhat severe, with those angular cheekbones and startling blue eyes.

When she reached me, I moved forward to hug her. Then I paused. I hadn't hugged anyone in a long time, and anyway, she'd always been a strange person to hug: when you reached for her, you could feel her whole body stiffen. So, instead, I just waved, feeling oddly wooden, and she gave me a vague and somewhat distant smile.

"Is that her?" she asked, nodding toward my daughter. I nodded. I realized Anna was the only one of my friends who had ever met my daughter.

Anna smiled, and the creases around her eyes softened her face. I felt myself warming to her again. I remembered sitting with her by that glowing kidney of a pool in Austin; I remembered going to shows with her under those strands of lights, drinking wine with her and watching *The Bachelor*, holding her hand in the waiting room of that doctor's office. I asked her how she was.

"Good, actually," she said. "I'm pregnant."

"Oh!" I said. I glanced at her belly. I wasn't entirely surprised—I had wondered whether that was her news when she called me—but it still shocked me a little. I wondered whether I would ever not feel envious of pregnant women, whether I would ever not feel like someone who has just lost a baby, someone sitting in a waiting room after seeing the enormous gap in their belly. Even now, pregnant again, I realized I was envying her, as though she had something I couldn't have, or something I had and knew I would lose. As though there weren't enough babies to go around, and one woman's pregnancy increased the chance of another woman's pregnancy loss. Or as though another woman's preparation to go off to the isolated but remarkable planet of pregnancy and birth meant it was time for me to come home from my own stint on my own planet.

"Oh, Anna," I said, "that's great! How far along?"

"Twelve weeks," she said. "I wanted to wait to tell you until I felt safe. But we've done all the testing, and it looks as though everything's healthy."

"I'm so happy for you," I said.

She nodded. There was something oddly distant about her smile: it was either beatific, that beatific smile women get when they're pregnant, or else very stoned. "I'm sorry I fell out of touch," she said. "I just—I felt like such a downer. I wanted to wait until I had some good news."

"Oh, you weren't ever a downer," I said, and didn't correct her about having fallen out of touch, though in fact I'd been the one who ignored her repeated attempts to make contact. "Really, Anna, that's just so terrific."

At the counter, we both ordered iced tea, and while we waited for it to brew, I asked her how she was feeling. "Better now," she said. "For a while I was so nauseous." She told me that, for several months, she hadn't been able to eat cheese. I told her that wasn't nausea. She laughed. When our iced tea came, we sat on the barrier wall between the stores and the splash pad where my daughter was playing, and she told me about the process of getting pregnant: how, after she'd miscarried that viable egg, she'd felt as though she was losing her mind. How the only thing that kept her sane was continuing the attempt to have a baby. She was persistent, she said, and thank God. Never before had she understood how blessed she had been to be born with a scientist's native obstinance.

I smiled. "Like Frankenstein," I said, remembering how often she'd used the book as a point of reference. "But instead of making a man, you're making a baby."

"Let's hope," she said. "It would be alarming if a man came out of me."

I laughed, then asked her if she knew whether it was a girl or a boy. Girl, she said, smiling at her iced tea. Then, without looking up, she asked if I wanted to have another baby. The question caught me off guard. I realized I should probably tell her I was pregnant. But it was still so early, eleven and a half weeks. And I'd told her last time, just before I'd learned about losing the pregnancy.

Clearly, this time was different. I'd had my eight-week appointment already, and I'd seen the heartbeat: that little heartbeat you hear first—*whoosh whoosh whoosh*—then see, the tiny chest of your baby stretching. My husband had been with me. He'd held my hand, and my eyes had welled with tears, so relieved I was not to be having another miscarriage, not to be seeing another one of those empty gray skies. At the end of the appointment, the technician had given me a picture of the baby: just a little gummy bear, but still. I'd heard the heart beating; I'd seen it rise and fall in the baby's chest. At home, I had the picture propped up on my desk.

Thinking about that photograph, I nearly told her, but still: something made me bite my tongue. I told myself I should wait until the official twelve weeks. So then I shrugged, and told Anna we were thinking about trying. I said we were considering it, but I was nervous about another hemorrhage, or another miscarriage.

Anna nodded. "Well, when you do," she said, "you should really consider embryo screening at least."

And there, again, was the return of that scientific superiority I'd noticed in Austin, when she was telling me about the ways you could avoid having a miscarriage: her offensive way of using that teacherly voice to tell me about having a baby. That way, she was saying, "you'll know that the embryo you're implanting is viable. Then you won't have to wait, if in the end it's not going to work. You might still have a miscarriage, of course, but it won't happen at eight weeks."

I took a sip of my iced tea, watched my daughter running dutifully in and out of the fountains. Truly, Anna was saying, I don't understand why anyone gets pregnant the old way anymore. How many women spend years of their lives—an enormous portion of their adult lives—having one miscarriage after the next? And they don't have to, or they wouldn't, if they harvested their eggs and screened the embryos.

I nodded and kept my mouth on the straw. A wave of nausea had started to build, and it was difficult for me to think of anything interesting to say in response. But my nod must have seemed like agreement, because Anna was going on with her lecture. She was saying how the old way was medieval: how, if all women harvested their eggs and screened their embryos, we could prevent most miscarriages. How we could lower rates of preeclampsia and hemorrhage.

I said something about how it was a good idea, but, really, I was focusing on not feeling nauseous. I kept my attention on my daughter, who was still working away in the splash pad, entirely absorbed in completing her cycles.

In the background, Anna was saying that here we were, in a country where sheep have been cloned, still giving birth as though we were living in the seventeenth century. She was reminding me that we had the worst maternal mortality rate of any developed country; that, if you were Black, or Native, the risk was downright murderous: far worse than driving, closer in fact to joining the air force. But that really, for anyone, pregnancy in this country was something out of the history books. No one does any trials on pregnant women, she said. I mean, no one does any trials on women; their hormones are too complicated. But they especially don't do any trials on women who have gotten pregnant, out of fear of harming the fetus. When it comes to pregnancy, we know about what we did a hundred years ago. Pregnancy involves travel backward in time to earlier eras of medicine.

It was, she went on, a bad state of affairs, and it wasn't improving at all. Global warming and pollution were making it worse. Women in Bangladesh were facing lower fertility rates than ever before as a result of increased salinity in the water. And not just there, but everywhere on Earth, for reasons that were still not completely clear, miscarriage rates were higher than ever before in history, and so were difficult, life-threatening births, and yet we refused to educate women on the dangers involved in pregnancy.

Of course, she continued, many women don't want to get pregnant. And why, if you don't want to have a child, should you have to carry around eggs that, for you, are nothing more than a terrible risk of life turning out in a way you hoped it wouldn't, a way that might ruin your life, a way that might even prove to be fatal? Why, she wanted to know, should a woman who doesn't want to get pregnant have to go through her life with a body full of hundreds of thousands of risks, when the technology was available for her to avoid it?

Now Anna paused in her lecture, as though waiting for me to agree. She had not always been such a lecturer. I wondered whether the last year and a half of quarantine had aggravated that aspect of her personality. Regardless, I found it abrasive, and also, I was so nauseous. Listening to her holding forth, I felt truly awful. I couldn't believe that I'd agreed to come here to meet her.

I felt her wanting me to look at her, but I kept my eyes on my daughter. She was still running in the fountains when, suddenly, heading toward us with the same absolute focus, she lurched forward and sprawled over the pavement. By the time I'd gotten to her and picked her up, she was sobbing in that way she occasionally did, when it seemed to me that she was not only frightened and hurt, but also betrayed: betrayed that the world she'd trusted to be gentle had turned out to be so treacherous.

In such moments, my daughter didn't cling to me: instead, she seemed to want to push me away, as though she had seen, in that instant, that I was of the world that had betrayed her. I glanced at Anna. She was stricken, obviously upset. Then I turned back to comforting my daughter. It took her a little while to calm down: first I had to get her to stop trying to escape me; then I had to get her to be willing to receive comfort. By then, I was sitting on a bench with her in my arms, and Anna was sitting next to me. The scrape on my daughter's forehead had stopped bleeding, though now the skin around it had swollen, rounded into the shape of an egg. My daughter was limp in my arms, exhausted from the effort of sobbing.

"God," Anna said. "It's terrifying. Having a child; it must be so scary. I mean, even that, just seeing her fall."

I thought of the moment she'd fallen. In that instant, a sudden contraction of pain had spread through me from the deepest part of my abdomen, a reaction so physical and so deeply internal that the temptation to call it maternal empathy would have been wrong: it was, instead, only selfish, only self-involved, a feeling of hers that I had made my own. A feeling that had nothing to do with the scrape she'd experienced on her forehead. Realizing that this was how I would react, if not always then at least sometimes, to my daughter's pain, I felt a wave of pity for her: such a splendid and utterly independent creature, given such a self-involved mother.

"I know," I said. "She was being so brave."

"And head injuries are no joke," Anna said. "What if she got a concussion?"

I kissed my daughter's head, then stroked her silky hair. In the background, Anna was going on about the dangers of concussions, and telling me there were, in fact, ways of minimizing the risks. She was saying there were genes associated with concussion susceptibility and recovery.

Really, she said, if you're interested, there are ways of minimizing so many of the risks that kids are facing these days, now more than ever. Covid and flu, smoke inhalation, anxiety, the effects of high salinity. It's harder at her age, but in utero, really, all those things are possible. Really, if you think about it, it's outrageous: here we are sending kids into a world full of so many new risks, and we're not doing any of the things we have the capability to do in order to prepare them. It's as though we imagine it's part of the experience, as though we *appreciate* or even *enjoy* that part of the experience: having a child, exposing them to risk, feeling good about ourselves if we shepherd them through it.

Sitting there next to Anna, holding my daughter in my arms, I felt myself growing angry. Was she saying that, by not genetically modifying my daughter, I had—for my own selfish purposes—decided to send her into a world full of new risks, but unprepared, without the resources she'd need to survive them? And what about the child I was pregnant with now? This one, too, I was failing, by deciding to conceive them without the assistance of science?

And what of the utterly dispensable risk of miscarriage? Had that miscarriage I'd had been for nothing? Had I chosen that risk, in order to feel better about getting pregnant? Had that risk been totally pointless, like the totally pointless pain of labor, something I'd once imagined was important, natural, and even useful, something that would prepare me, eventually, for the arrival of my daughter? In one stroke, Anna had demolished that logic. But that wasn't even the worst part of the lecture. It was one thing for her to tell me how much unnecessary risk—of miscarriage, of hemorrhage—I was exposing myself to, but quite another for her to tell me that I'd essentially harmed my daughter by choosing not to modify her.

Here she was, a woman who didn't have an actual child

yet, a woman who'd had a miscarriage but only after a few measly days of pregnancy, telling me that there was no reason to risk any of what I'd risked, and no reason for my child to shoulder any of the risks I'd asked her to shoulder.

I was so angry I couldn't really hear her anymore, though she was still talking about the risks that could be eliminated through genetic modification of embryos, and by now my daughter had calmed enough to wriggle sideways in my arms so that she could stare at Anna. She was sucking her thumb, staring at Anna, until she removed her thumb and said, "Cwack."

I blinked at her. "Like a duck?" I said.

"No, no," she said, getting cross, "cwack, cwack, cwack."

"Oh," I said. "Crackers." I smiled falsely at Anna. "She's hungry. I should get her home for a snack."

"Totally," Anna said. I'd interrupted her speech. Her face was a little bit flushed. She seemed suddenly aware of having gone on too long, or perhaps of having gone on with too little awareness of the actual child, unmodified, who was sitting next to her. In that moment, I hated her.

Then I wondered why I was worrying about her. I had a daughter to feed. A daughter who would face risks I couldn't yet comprehend. I had a daughter to look after.

"Oh, Anna," I said, making my voice as friendly as possible, just wanting to get the interaction over with. "I'm so happy you're pregnant."

I reached forward to give her a hug. She received it somewhat stiffly. "I can't wait to meet your baby," I said.

"Thanks," she said. "I'm happy you're here. It makes moving easier."

# 10.

WE HEADED HOME, my daughter and I, and did not stop in the Museum of Natural History, where we usually stopped so that my daughter could run through the bird hall, and open the drawers full of dead red-winged blackbirds, or run down the ramp from the Laysan Island Cyclorama, full of the cries of seabirds mourning their own extinction, past the glass case with the arrested wave of migrating songbirds, all the way to the case full of bird's eggs: row upon row of eggs, from the elliptical moon of an ostrich egg to the little blue egg of the American robin. I always found it strange to see the robin's egg so perfectly preserved in that case: in my own life, I'd so often seen those eggs broken in the grass, the blue nearly translucent in the spring sunshine, and often smeared with a little bright red, sometimes with a little pink fetus curled compactly inside one of the halves. In the museum, however, there was the same egg, but still whole, and still perfect. I liked visiting the museum with my daughter, especially since it was always empty, so I didn't worry about exposing her to Covid. But on that morning after we met up with Anna, I felt too nauseous to go in.

Instead, we walked past it and the old capitol building with its glistening gold dome, along the polluted Iowa River, over the pale blue pedestrian bridge. The river gleamed in the sunlight, but it also smelled awful, and I could see something pink and fleshy floating under the bridge. Last winter, our neighbor had been out for a walk when she discovered the dead body of a young woman floating past. I looked away from the water. The nausea was really bad, but if I didn't look at the river, and if I walked with my hat pulled low over my eyes, I could keep it under control.

It was best for the nausea if I didn't think: not about how Anna had gotten pregnant if she'd miscarried her viable embryo; not about what she'd said about how all women should "at least" screen their embryos for viability; not about the lecture on risks you could prevent, of concussion, of flu, of anxiety, of damage as a result of smoke inhalation and salinity.

Thinking about embryos at all, in fact, made the nausea rise precipitously, so I tried not to, and I also tried not to feel angry: not about Anna's certainty that the right thing to do was to engineer embryos to make them invulnerable to risk, though of course the best way to make embryos invulnerable to risk would be not to make them at all.

It was as though she imagined life could be free from risk, if you had enough scientific acumen, if you had the resources. And, having reached that conclusion, she had decided that to have a child and expose them to risk was immoral. What sort of reverse Frankenstein approach was she taking, I wondered, this insane refusal to abandon a creature to any sort of risk at all, this crazed determination to protect a child from any possible imperfect outcome?

She was wrong, I thought to myself. She was wrong, not me—but the more indignant I got, the more nauseous I felt, and so I tried not to think about Anna. I tried, instead, to focus on what was around me as I pushed the stroller home: the old art museum, which had flooded one too many times and had been left empty, the sycamore trees with their bark peeling away to reveal new wood in a hallucinatory shade of lime green. I pushed the stroller up the hill behind the shiny new art building, past the house with the orchard and the house with the raspberry patch, and finally turned right down our street.

I didn't think about Anna until I'd put my daughter down for her nap. Then I lay down for a nap of my own: one of those hideous naps into the depths of which I'd been drawn every day in those early weeks of my pregnancy; one of those naps I struggled to wake from and had to use all my remaining strength to pull myself up and out of, so that afterward, awake, I felt more tired than I had before falling asleep.

Once I'd forced myself to get up, I sat for a while with my head in my hands and recalled what I'd been dreaming about: once again, the sonogram that had caught my missed miscarriage. The cloudy sky, the missing baby who had been reabsorbed, the vast, gray-and-white expanse of emptiness. I'd dreamed that I'd been flying in that sky, or perhaps swimming, since the air had had a quality of density. So I was swimming, then, pushing the air away with my hands, and looking around for a lost baby.

Then I remembered what Anna had said. That all women should, at least, screen their embryos for viability. At least? What else was there to do? What else had she done? How had she gotten pregnant, if she'd miscarried her viable embryo? I didn't know. I couldn't think. And it was so hard to get up. I was so nauseous. I felt, I really did, just as I'd felt in that dream: as though I was swimming through some sort of horribly dense air, trying to break out into the open.

# 11.

I GOT THROUGH the rest of the weekend in the same way—pulling myself through the same nauseating viscosity—and on Monday I had my twelve-week appointment. I went alone. I had been reassured by the eight-week appointment, when I'd seen the heartbeat, and by the sonogram pictures they'd given me of that little gummy-bear shaped baby. Then, once again, the darkened room, and the bright screen, and the warm gel on my belly. The comforting feeling of the sonogram wand getting rolled over my skin; chatting happily with the technician.

And then, once again: her sudden silence. And the gray caves and cliffs on the screen. And my realization that I didn't hear the sound of the heartbeat. I started breathing harder. "Do you not see anything?" I said. "Is the baby not there?"

"Well," she said quietly, "I don't hear a heartbeat."

Then I started crying. Quietly, at first, just tears rolling out of my eyes. The technician noticed, and asked me, gently, if I wanted a break. Then, perhaps because of her kindness, perhaps because the last technician hadn't asked me if I wanted a break, I started really sobbing, and so she left the room for a while. I called my husband. He told me he'd come as soon as he could. The sonogram technician returned with another technician to double-check that there was really no heartbeat.

They both hovered there, moving the wand over my belly, making measurements on that cloudy screen. It was just like that other time, and yet different, because now I could see the baby, and last time there had been such awful emptiness.

"Do you want a picture of the baby?" one of them said. "Some women want one, to have as a keepsake."

There it was, up on the screen, the same little curled shape: the large head and the partial limbs. But this time it was perfectly still. Its chest didn't stretch for the heartbeat.

I told them I was okay with not having a picture. So they measured the baby for a while, while I whimpered, and then my husband came and held my hand until they'd finished, and when they'd left he hugged me. "I'm sorry, I'm just so sorry," I kept saying, over and over again, a senseless thing I couldn't keep myself from repeating.

# 12.

I DIDN'T TALK to Anna for a few weeks after that. I just didn't have time. I had to prepare for the D&C, in order to remove the remains of the baby. And so I'd gone under again, though this time only partially. You might be aware of the surgery, they told me, but afterward you won't remember it. Once again, then, the stainless-steel room, though this one wasn't so cold, and now I was sitting up, with my feet in the stirrups. Once again, the rush of doctors and nurses around me. And, once again, the administration of anesthetic, and the swift swoon into senselessness.

If I was aware of anything, even by the time the operation was over, I'd already forgotten it. All I could recall, when, somewhat disoriented, I looked around and realized they were telling me I was free to go home, and that, if I was able to stand, I could go to the bathroom and get dressed, was the moment when the needle full of sedative went in. And then someone squeezing my arm, and—for a moment—the resident who was performing the surgery laughing with the attending physician about what she called her "perfection-ism": there had been some extra, unnecessary precaution she'd taken. And then there had been one moment of trying, and failing, to check the time. I found the clock, but before I could read the hour, it slid down the wall and into utter emptiness.

Now, post-operation, they gave me a wax cup of water and a plastic bag of the clothes I'd been wearing. They asked if I could stand. I tried, wobbled, then corrected myself. Then I was in the bathroom, changing back into my clothes, look-ing up from the toilet at the sign that said if I'd been sexu-ally assaulted, it wasn't my fault. When I stumbled out of the bathroom, someone was waiting with a wheelchair, and someone else gave me a plastic bag. "A memento," they said, "from the nursing staff." I took it, and they wheeled me out to my husband, who wheeled me out to the parking garage.

When I climbed into the car, I realized I was still very high. It was difficult for me to pry open my eyes. I asked my husband to stop at the drugstore to pick up pads, since they'd promised the bleeding would be heavier than a period and given me instructions about not putting anything inside myself for a month.

At the drugstore, I waited in the car. Then I checked the contents of the plastic bag. It was a tiny white blanket, the size of a doll's blanket, and a little white votive candle with a card that said I could light it for my baby's sake. There was also a little silver charm the card said I could wear close to my heart.

Deeply stoned, with my head propped against the car window, I blinked at these items for a few moments. Then I fell asleep and didn't wake up until my husband was helping me up the stairs and into our bedroom.

# 13.

SEVERAL HOURS LATER, I woke. I was in no pain, and perfectly free of the nausea that had been with me for months. It was simple, easy, to pull myself out of bed. I no longer felt as though I was dragging myself up from the darkest depths of the ocean.

I wasn't even bleeding at all. Totally free of all symptoms, I felt a little euphoric: free, at last, from my days of pregnancy.

I got up and walked through the empty house. My husband had taken our daughter out. Alone, free, I almost felt happy. And yet: in each room I moved through, there was an eeriness. These were the rooms where, for three months, I'd waited for our new baby. For three months, though I was so nauseous it was difficult for me to read, or look at my computer, or do any work, I had told myself that I needed to relax. This was what I needed to do to take care of our baby.

Now, there was no chair I could sit in that was not the chair where I'd waited for the arrival of our little baby. There was no couch; there were no windows. By night, I felt as though I couldn't spend another day in that house. And so, after I put our daughter to sleep, my husband and I made last-minute plans to go to Chicago.

We booked a hotel we couldn't really afford. It was our first outing since our daughter was born. We made dinner reservations. We were giddy, thrown into the excitement of all this sudden planning. We left the next day, leaving the whole pregnancy episode behind us: there in that house, in which we'd been confined since the start of the pandemic.

It was a riotously clear, cool day in July. The sun was outrageously blue. Our daughter was a dream in the car: eating crackers, kicking her feet, singing songs she'd recently invented. We brought the dog. The four of us went to the beach. I couldn't swim, because my cervix was still open, so there was a risk of infection, but I waded up to my ankles and watched while my husband threw our daughter up into the bright blue sky, and caught her as her ankles splashed into the water. The little dog ran back and forth in the sand, and for a moment I felt so far away from my life. I felt as though perhaps we had not only traveled to Chicago, perhaps this was not Lake Michigan, but perhaps, instead, I had voyaged with my husband and our child to another time, another continent. As though we had come, perhaps, to Lake Geneva, as Shelley did with her husband and her own child, that summer when she conceived of her monster.

But it was a movie version of that summer, a bright and sunny version, a version that ignored the historical facts: the lost child, the ash-clotted skies. Everything was so bright and so blue. Later, we walked through the park, us and everyone else out having picnics, enjoying that strangely fine slice of July, that ebb in the pandemic, a world in which there existed no evidence of anything bad, no sickness, no loss, nothing re-sembling tragedy. Our daughter walked along the city streets. On a Monday morning, we walked to the empty beach. The sun shone on the cracked, glazed surface of the endless gray water. Later, we went to the zoo. We had fancy coffee; we ate breakfast outside; she filled her mouth with blackberries.

And then we came home. I still wasn't bleeding, though they had promised I would. That afternoon, clearing the cooler out, I had the distinct thought that perhaps I wouldn't bleed at all: perhaps the surgery had miraculously removed every last trace of the pregnancy, and it was that night, after I put our daughter to bed, that I checked my computer and found a message from the hospital. I clicked on it. There was a chart: Abnormal, I saw, XXY. Male. Triploidy.

When I googled "triploidy," the first thing that came up was triploid carp. Somewhat dazed, a little light-headed, as though I'd gone too long without eating, I clicked on the link. Triploid carp, a gardening website informed me, are naturally infertile. They have three sets of chromosomes because sci-entists instantaneously freeze their developing egg, causing a mutation. This is done because carp are an invasive species that have caused enormous environmental damage in lakes and ponds and streams across the US, devouring all the local species, but they are also very good at consuming toxic algae that, as a result of pollution, have proliferated wildly. Caught between a rock and a hard place, scientists have found a way to make carp infertile. That way they won't be able to repro-duce, but you can also introduce them to your pond with the hopes that they'll clear out the otherwise uncontrollable algae.

For a little while, I looked at images of ponds full of fertile carp: there were pictures of ponds so full the carp were smashed together, so that the ponds seemed not to be full of water but instead full of carp. You could walk across those ponds, I thought, without ever once getting your shoes wet.

For a while, I gaped at those carp. Then I emerged from my stupor and re-googled "human triploidy." I learned that triploid babies, like triploid carp, have three sets of chromosomes. It happens when two sperm fertilize one egg at the same instant. These babies are, as every website was quick to say, "incompatible with human life." Usually, they abort within a few days, but sometimes they develop further. It is possible for them to develop heartbeats, though usually the heartbeat is weak, indetectable by ultrasound. In some very rare cases, they manage to develop a strong enough heartbeat to be detected, and in these rare cases, it is occasionally possible for them to stay alive until birth, though, after that, they will not survive for more than a few hours.

These babies, the ones who manage to survive until birth, have a particular phenotypical type: wide-set eyes, a cleft palate, webbed fingers, webbed toes. They die, the website told me, because their hearts are defective. And this, I realized, was what had happened to the baby I'd been carrying: a little boy with three sets of chromosomes, who had still, nevertheless, managed to develop a heartbeat strong enough to be detected.

At some point, however, his heartbeat must have stopped. Usually, this causes miscarriage to happen spontaneously. But my body had not wanted to let this little boy go. Even now, I still wasn't bleeding. Still, even after the surgery, my body did not want to release whatever traces remained of his body: his cleft palate, his wide-set eyes. His tiny webbed fingers and his tiny webbed toes.

I went downstairs and told my husband I'd gotten a message from the hospital. "Do you want to know the gender of the baby, and what went wrong?"

"No," he said.

We ate dinner on the screened-in porch behind our house. Beyond the screens, there was a garden, but, because of the screen, it was hard for me to make out the individual shapes of the leaves.

# 14.

THAT NIGHT, I couldn't sleep. I tossed and turned in the darkness, then finally got up and went downstairs. I went to the window and looked out. This was how I'd lived in the first year of our daughter's life, when I nursed her at night: awake while the others slept, going up and down the stairs. For a year, we kept a lamp on in the kitchen. Because I was always ravenous, I often stood in the light from the refrigerator, eating leftovers from dinner, gnawing chicken bones like Popsicles.

Now, the nights had been returned to darkness. I wasn't hungry. In the living room, I looked out windows to see the August trees, so fluid in the moonlight that they seemed like underwater plants. I watched them for a while, waving in the current, until I began to feel tired. Then I lay down on the couch, propped up on a pillow so that I could still see the trees waving outside. I began to drift in and out of sleep, the kind of sleep that your mind nearly succumbs to, then pulls itself out of at the last minute. But when your mind does pull itself out, it's so strangely weary that the living room begins to seem dreamlike, so I wasn't sure if I was dreaming or not when I got up off the couch, climbed out the window, and dove out into the darkness.

I swam for a while, breaststroke, with my eyes open, as though I was looking for someone. But it was he who found me. He appeared suddenly in the dark water, his face, like a little moon, made luminous by the murkiness from which he emerged. I recognized his wide-set eyes. His mouth, with the cleft palate, was serious and gentle. As soon as we met, as soon as we locked eyes, he turned and swam away. He parted the water with his webbed fingers.

I followed him. Immediately, without thinking, I followed him farther: not because I wanted to catch him and bring him home, but simply because a mother follows her son. And that's how I knew it wasn't real when I woke with the sun flooding the living room windows.

I knew I was dreaming when I climbed the stairs. I dreamed the bathroom, the tile, the toilet, the underwear around my knees. Overnight, I'd started to bleed. The first blood was gray. There, in my underwear, I found a piece of fish skin, no bigger than a postage stamp.

I looked at it for a while. It was rubbery and uncooked, silver-flecked. I held it between my thumb and my finger. Then I flushed it down the toilet.

• • •

# 15.

THAT MORNING, THERE was a new message from the hospital in my inbox. Once again, I clinked the link. Abnormal, I read. Villi, partial hydatidiform mole.

I googled "partial hydatidiform mole"—cyst-like tumors in the placenta; surgical removal; chemotherapy, etc.—then called the hospital and asked if I could speak with someone about my recent test results. Cheerfully, the nurse pulled up my file. "So," she said, "let's see. You're nearly four months pregnant."

For a moment, it seemed to me that if I said yes, my life might magically divert: exit its current state, move through that door in the universe that led into the life in which I was still pregnant.

"No," I said. "I had a D&C last week."

"Oh," she said, stricken. "Your file says you're still pregnant."

"I'm not," I said.

"I'm so sorry," she said. "I'm sorry, your file says you are. But, yes, now I see. Okay. Well. I'll need to get a doctor to talk to you about this."

And so I waited for a doctor to call me back. While I did, I spent some more time researching molar pregnancy. Until recently, I learned, tissue from miscarriages had not been regularly screened for cancerous material, which meant that molar pregnancies went undiagnosed, and also meant that it was not uncommon for a woman in her childbearing years, with a history of miscarriages, to arrive at the hospital one day with inoperable brain cancer, or metastatic myeloma, the cancerous material that had begun to proliferate in her uterus during pregnancy having now spread to every other part of her body.

I shut that window down. Then I spent some time on forums for women who have lost pregnancies, searching for "moles." These forums: they are enormous, throbbing sink-holes of grief. Many of these women have lost four or five pregnancies. They have invented a language of their own, an acronym code, TTN, BFN, MC, a shorthand for loss, shared among women who understand it. Some of their screen names include the number of children they've lost; some of them have named their lost babies. Their profiles list dates of those losses, and ages—in weeks—of their unborn.

Still waiting for the doctor to call back, I read the story of another woman who had been diagnosed with a partial mole. She had undergone a D&C to remove the cancerous material, then had been monitored for some time until it was determined it was safe for her to try to get pregnant again. Then she'd had another miscarriage. Then she'd had another pregnancy that was also diagnosed as a molar pregnancy. Then another D&C. Then another pregnancy, in which the sonogram had revealed an embryo with "four-times-normal nuchal folds": this one died at eight weeks.

Some women, I thought, experience their reproductive years as a time of joy and plenty; others move through them in fear of an unwanted pregnancy. For other women still, those years are a revolving door between losses. It was un-pleasant, that forum: those women who, presumably, went to work during the day and tried to pretend all was well, then came home to report on the forum. Unpleasant, but I felt at home there, or at least more at home than I felt with people who glowed about the joys of pregnancy, or with Anna, who had regaled me with all the ways to remove risk from the state of being pregnant.

As though it were a choice. As though I'd chosen risk, when in fact I could have chosen safety. As though I'd chosen to do this dangerously.

Then the doctor called. She told me that, in addition to the embryo, small tumors had been growing in my placenta. Or really, "the placenta was itself a cluster of tumorous cells, which were growing out of control, and eventually overtook the pregnancy."

Those tumors, she said, had been surgically removed during the D&C. Hopefully, they'd gotten them all. Still, however, I'd have to be monitored every week for the return of potentially cancerous material. Once my HCG levels had returned to zero for three weeks in a row, I could be monitored monthly. After three months, if all went well, I could try again to have a baby, though the risk of another molar pregnancy and the return of potentially invasive cancerous material would now be higher than it had been before the initial molar pregnancy.

# 16.

IT WAS THAT afternoon that the bleeding started for real. I bled and I bled. I bled with such wild abandon. Two nights in a row, I bled through the pad and my underwear and my shorts and the sheets and into the mattress, then spent the next day scrubbing it, and drying it with a fan, which drew more blood up from inside the mattress, so that clean or at least faint spots of brownish peach would be deep red again by the end of the day.

All day and all night, I felt like Lady Macbeth: no matter what I did, everything around me was still bloody. In the morning, when I cracked an egg for my breakfast, there were three spots of blood. That afternoon, when I went to the garden to pick a bell pepper to slice for my daughter's lunch, I walked along the row of pepper plants and realized that, here in the garden, green wombs were growing on trees.

Back in the kitchen, I sliced one open. There was the green carp; there the white placenta. It was bristling with seeds, one of which had grown large, and was swelling into a little bell pepper. I pulled the whole thing out with two thumbs and threw it in the garbage disposal.

Life, I thought, is full of murder. In her highchair, my daughter was calling for lunch. I took it over. The same fly that had been inside our house for a week was buzzing at the windows. "Why, why, why," my daughter said, pointing up at the fly. I spun around and slapped the glass.

My daughter, surprised, started crying. She'd been buzzing with that fly all week. "Oh, shh," I said, "don't worry." I was hiding the corpse in the palm of my hand. "Everything's fine. I'm just taking him outside to play with his friends."

That night, once again, I couldn't sleep. I lay awake on that mattress so recently soaked with blood and realized that, during those months of nausea, I hadn't been tenderly caring for my little seed of a creature, caring for him for as long as

I was given him to take care of: no, I'd been growing tumors, and those had overtaken the baby.

My body, I realized, had eaten my child alive. His rare and miraculous heart hadn't stopped; no, my womb had consumed him. Lying there, I could feel the blood sliding out of me. I could feel it parting me, warm, creeping out, everything that remained within from that episode of killing my growing baby.

Suddenly I remembered: when I was a child, we had pet rabbits. Sometimes, the girl rabbits would get pregnant. Then their bodies would swell, and they'd become strange to themselves. They'd spend their time in the corner of the hutch, nervously eyeing all the other rabbits. Then they didn't want to be held. At some point, after some duration of weeks, they gave birth to a litter of little bald and blind babies. And sometimes, in the mornings, we'd go down to check on them and the babies were gone, and the nest was all bloody. We'd realize the mother bunny had eaten her babies.

Is this, I wondered, how our rabbits felt, the night after they'd eaten their young? Did they lie in their bloody nests and think, what have I become? I always felt bad for those rabbits. There they were, only one or two years old, and suddenly they'd given birth to six babies. Suddenly, without anyone to explain what had happened or what they should do next, they were lying on their sides with six babies jostling to find another one of their nipples.

Perhaps it was understandable that they'd eaten those babies. Perhaps it was perfectly natural. But then, surely, neither had anyone prepared them for what happened next: the silence, and the total abandon. The fact that you can't return to what you were before your babies were born, and before you failed to nurture them.

Then I remembered our family dog. Our little girl: sweet and brown-eyed, she'd slept at the foot of the bed. We'd held her in our laps. She had thirty stuffed toys. She didn't require a leash, but followed us, right at our heels, if we ever left the house. My mother, overcome with love and the desire to keep her, had decided to breed her. We had taken her to a farm; we watched while a male dog mounted her while she tried to escape, and failed, and looked up at us with her sweet brown eyes, totally confused as to why we'd exposed her to such inexplicable brutality.

Later, the vet confirmed she was pregnant. But instead of a litter, she was only carrying a single baby. It was as though she'd so believed she was human, that she was our actual child, that her mind persuaded her body to reproduce as a human would.

She went into labor one night around dinner. All night, she labored. My mother stayed awake with her. By the morning, my mother was crying. The dog still hadn't given birth. Finally, the vet's office opened, so we took her in, and the vet used forceps to pull out the baby: the single baby that had gotten so big he was nearly the same size as his mother.

From that day on, the mother was different. For one thing, she had no interest in the puppy she'd given birth to. She turned away from her creature. All day, the puppy pawed at her. He was only trying to get milk, but he was so big: every time he tried, he nearly knocked her over.

The mother dog—our little girl—spent all her time trying to get away from him, while looking up at us guiltily. She knew we wanted her to take care of her baby. And so, for us, she did her best. But she really wanted to get away from that puppy, and so, at some point, she also started trying to get away from us.

She just wanted to be alone. Sometimes, at night, when the puppy was asleep, we cuddled with her on the couch. Then she was still our little girl. But most of the time, everything was entirely different. She was older and more alone. Slight sounds startled her out of her solitude. She eyed us all with wariness. Even her own body had become different. She had hip problems from that day on, and couldn't play, and eventually she didn't want to go on walks anymore. It was hard for her to get up. Finally, my parents put her to sleep, and buried her in the yard.

Or so I recalled, lying on top of my bloody mattress. I gave up on going to sleep. Then I went downstairs and made myself a mug of warm milk. Holding my mug, I stood at the window looking out at the crescent moon, the moon that had once been full, but now seemed as though an enormous scoop had been taken out of it. Faintly, ever so faintly, you could see the ghost of the missing circle.

Then I remembered a girl I knew in high school. She'd gotten pregnant. We never knew how. It was a subject of incessant rumor. We all knew, though she'd only told one or two of her friends. Under our curious gaze, she started wearing bigger and bigger clothes, and then she was out of school for a month. Then it was summer vacation. At the end of the break, she had the baby.

Someone I knew, who was friends with her friends, told me she'd given the baby up for adoption. She came back for our senior year. She was back to her old clothes, but she wasn't the same. She didn't go to any parties, and she didn't participate in any school activities. It was as though some part of her had exited the life she'd led up to that point, though her body was still moving through it.

Maybe she'd found her way back to her old life at some point. Maybe now she was grateful that she'd had that baby. I didn't know. I didn't keep up with her; I didn't keep up with anyone from that high school. Or so I thought, standing at the window, gathering and illustrating in my mind a catalogue of monstrosities, all the abandoned babies, all the abandoned young mothers, whose bodies, uninformed, had to move blind through the state of pregnancy.

At some point, I vaguely remembered, while I was recovering from the D&C, the Supreme Court had upheld the most recent abortion ban out of Texas: the one that permitted private citizens to sue people if they helped a woman get an abortion. Standing there at the window, three pregnancies and a hundred years away from that apartment where I'd been sued for other reasons in Austin, I could see the moon sinking down toward the tops of the trees like one of those claws in the arcade game where you try to pick up a fuzzy toy.

Then the moon disappeared. Through the gaps in the foliage that remained as a result of the derecho, I could see blood spreading up from beyond the horizon. That law in Texas had been upheld, and my body, taking its right to end a pregnancy into its own hands, had consumed a second baby.

· · ·

# 17.

ALL THIS TIME, Anna had been calling me. She'd called five or six times, and she'd even left two messages, but I couldn't bring myself to call her back.

Perhaps part of my resistance to seeing her had to do with the fact that she was still pregnant, while my own state of existence had so radically shifted. Or perhaps it had to do with the fact that, once again, I had seen her so shortly before learning that my own pregnancy had ended, so that it almost seemed as though seeing her had been the error that ended not only that time, the time when I hoped to have another baby, but also the time before that, the capsule of time when I was alone with my husband and our child, and we gardened, and watched the trees, and planned to have another baby.

Or perhaps it was the fact that I'd chosen to have a baby naturally, chosen to expose myself to all the risks she'd lectured me about when we were watching my daughter run in the fountains, and the choice had turned out to be wrong. My child, as it turned out, had been faced with too many risks. In fact, he hadn't survived them.

It could have been any of those reasons that caused me to avoid Anna. We were, furthermore, entering a bad stage of the pandemic again. Cases were rising alarmingly all over the country, as a result of the low rate of vaccination. The hospital down the street from us, the same hospital where my husband and I had received our rabies vaccination at an entirely different time in history, was full past capacity once again; they were turning away mild heart attacks.

Once again, we could hear the medevac helicopters coming and going overhead all through the day and at all hours of night. In order to protect vulnerable students, some school districts had proposed mask mandates. Now, in front of these schools, enormous anti-mask protests were occurring every day. If you drove past them, you could see anti-mask Iowan men and women holding signs that read, "My Body, My Choice."

At the university, where I taught, the president had made a statement confirming that, to protect such students' rights, they would not require students to get vaccines or to wear masks, and they would require that all instructors teach their classes in person, with no exceptions, not even in the case of instructors who had complicating health conditions such as asthma, or heart disease, or pregnancy.

So now, after two years online, I was preparing to go back to work again. I waited until the weekend before classes began to finally go back to my office, and when I unlocked my door, I felt as though I were entering an abandoned submarine, or a civilization preserved under lava. The calendar was still turned to March 2020; my drawers were still full of plastic bags for pumped breast milk, since at that time I'd just come back to work after my maternity leave and was still frantically pumping in the fifteen minutes I had between classes. There was a petrified tea bag in my thermos; there was a used paper towel crumpled up on my desk.

Someone had left this office in a state of distress, I thought to myself. It had been abandoned many years ago. Now, returning from space, I was finding evidence of the last human beings. That civilization—the world in which I'd gone to work with my pink breast pump in its black bag, tired because my daughter woke three times during the night—seemed like something lost hundreds of thousands of years ago. And, returning there, I was leaving the planet where my husband and I had gone with our baby.

I didn't want to. I didn't want those years to slip away. I went home as soon as I could, and that weekend, I didn't think to call Anna.

# 18.

THE FOLLOWING THURSDAY, I went to the hospital for my first blood draw. The night before, I'd dreamed another pregnancy: this baby, inspired by that grieving woman online, had "eight-times-normal" nuchal folds. My baby, unlike hers, survived: he was born a happy, healthy bulldog puppy. What joy I felt in that dream: to be playing with him in the yard, nuzzling him close, feeling his warm wet tongue on my forearm.

In the morning, still dazed by that dream-happiness, I walked to the hospital. It was sunny and cool. Somehow, I felt hopeful. Inside the hospital, however, the hope immediately started to ebb. Masked, I checked in, then followed the same route to the Women's Health Center—three long halls, the elevator marked M—and checked in again: this was where they charged the ten-dollar copay.

I remembered it, once again: the return of the copay once you're no longer carrying a living baby. In Montana, the fees had returned as soon as the embryo had died: eight thousand dollars for the surgery to remove it. Here, at least, the surgery had been covered. Ten dollars was nothing. And yet it still seemed to broadcast such a clear message: here is how much we support you when you're carrying a potential baby; here is how much we support you when the baby is gone. When it's just you and your flawed woman's body.

I reported to the waiting room. All around me, the women were pregnant. They were there, glowing and round, accompanied by their doting spouses. Why, I wondered again, can't they set aside a waiting room for the unhappy women? The women who have lost pregnancies, or the women who didn't want to get pregnant? People forget, I thought, that in addition to being a site of great joy, these offices are also a location of devastation.

And yet there we all were, waiting together. It was nearly an hour before they called me back. The nurse weighed me, took my pulse, and promised that the doctor would be in soon. Much later, when he came, I was surprised to find that they'd sent me a young boy. He couldn't have been much more than twenty. He checked my file, knitted his brow, then scolded me for not already having gotten my blood drawn. The nurse came in and apologized, then gave me directions to the laboratory.

And so it was pass go again, and down another hall to another windowless laboratory, where they bound my arm with elastic and pricked the needle in and I noticed that there were fluorescent panels on the ceiling: hot-air balloons and hummingbirds and fire trucks.

The technician told me they were from the old children's blood lab. At first, I was confused: Was there, in fact, a lab set aside for old children? What qualified as an old child? Then

I realized it was the lab that had been old. The technician was explaining that they'd redone it, added windows, made it more cheerful, obliterated the need for panels of fluorescent lights, but before they'd thrown them out, she'd asked them to send her the panels. She told me the light helped her get through the winter. "Yes," I said, "I see," and then I was back in the waiting room with the pregnant women and the proud spouses, then back with the boy in his scrubs, and he was checking my chart again, and telling me I'd have to get my hormone levels down to zero for three weeks in a row before the scans could move from weekly to monthly, and then I'd be scanned for a year, and in the meantime it would be prohibitively dangerous to get pregnant.

"The last person told me three months," I said.

"It's a year," he said, with an exaggeratedly apologetic wince. Then he asked me what I planned to use for birth control.

It had been years since I'd thought about birth control. I couldn't even remember what I used to do to avoid getting pregnant. Vaguely, I suggested the rhythm method.

The doctor scoffed. That, he told me, wasn't birth control. He told me I could choose between the pill or an IUD.

"No," I said. For years, I had been doing everything I could—reading blogs, taking vitamins, drinking raspberry tea—to make sure my hormones were working perfectly in order to either get pregnant with or give birth to or breastfeed a baby. I didn't want to now rearrange my hormones in order to prevent a pregnancy. Plus, online, I'd learned so much about the dangers of hormonal birth control, how little research had been done into its long-term effects on women's health, or its short- and long-term effects on women's psychology, or on their personalities.

The doctor looked at me with growing hardness. He was looking at me, I realized, as I might have looked at someone who refused to get the Covid vaccine: like someone who was monstrously opposed to standard science. "If your HCG levels rise," he told me, "we'll need to start chemotherapy."

"I won't get pregnant," I said. Then I asked him again how long I needed to wait before trying, how long until there was less risk of the tumors returning. I was hoping that this time the answer would be different.

"It's a year," he said, again.

I told him I was thirty-nine, and that if I waited that long, I might not be able to get pregnant. I asked him if he would double-check with another doctor. I thought I saw him narrow his eyes. "Sure," he said. Then he checked my vital signs. I leaned forward; he came behind me and pressed his stethoscope into my back. I took a shallow breath. Then, finally, he left to double-check with the attending physician.

Forty-five minutes later, he opened the door and poked his head in. "It's six months," he said. Then he was off. I passed reception on my way out. They said I owed another ten dollars for the blood draw. I started to give them a credit card, but they told me they already had one on file. Great, I said, then headed down another long hallway.

When I finally made it outside, it had started raining. Here there were no glowing hot-air balloons, no glowing birds. Everything was gray and unillumined, a warm, rainy day in late August. This was not the moon. This was not the Arctic. My crew of doctors had refused to go on. We had turned back toward more temperate climates.

The expedition doomed, I walked for a while, got wet, started quietly crying. Then I called my husband to ask him to come get me, but he didn't pick up. Then I saw another missed call from Anna.

# 19.

SHE DROVE ME the long way home so that I could have time to stop crying. We drove past the emergency room, then past the power plant, then over the river. She took another turn, and another, and then we were driving past the Emma Goldman Clinic, and the prayer vigil that gathered there every day, and the counterprotest, where this time it was women who were holding signs that read, "My Body, My Choice." Then I remembered Anna standing in her apartment, telling me how she'd driven to the Planned Parenthood that had been closed, and how she'd stood there, not knowing what to do.

The rain had picked up again. The river was gray. We crossed it, and I had stopped crying, but Anna turned into the park. We passed the picnic pavilions: no picnics today.

Anna parked. "I'm really sorry," she said.

I was grateful to her for not having asked why I didn't tell her I was pregnant. Why, though we'd shared so much, or she'd shared so much with me, I'd kept another secret from her.

"I'm sorry I haven't called," I said. "It's just been such a hard couple of weeks."

"It's okay," she said. "I understand."

"How are you?" I asked. "How's the baby?"

She touched her stomach. She was showing now. She was wearing a jumpsuit that swelled around her belly, and her arms and face were softer than they had been. I thought of the softness that comes with pregnancy, and the softness afterward: the swollen breasts, the extra skin around your stomach. The looser hips. The way your body has changed to accommodate a little baby. Sometimes, over the last year and a half, that softness had frustrated me: once, I'd tried to go for a run and my whole body had felt wrong, as though my limbs, unspooled by labor, had been hung together again, but less carefully.

Now, when I looked at myself in the mirror, I didn't always love the dark stripe that remained on my belly, or the way my stomach swelled more than it once had. Other days, however, as I never had in the past, I felt such love for my body. I loved the way my nipples were darker: they had changed to make it easier for my daughter to find them at night. They had become beacons for her little mouth.

During the months and years of my daughter's baby-hood, when I looked in the mirror, I saw a body that fed her. Seeing that, I liked my body more than I ever had when I was younger, when I thought my body was there for other purposes. After my daughter was born, those other purposes began to recede. Then my body was for picking my daughter up; it was for her head when she wanted to rest; it was for waiting to become pregnant again.

And now what? Now what was to become of my body? For six months, or maybe even a year, I'd have to wait before I could try to get pregnant. Then I'd be forty. At that point, given the trouble I'd already had, and since now the chances of having another molar pregnancy were higher, it was probably unlikely that it would happen at all. And that was if everything went well with the scans: if not, a year of chemotherapy.

At the very least, I'd have to let go of the certainty that I'd have another baby. I'd have to go back to life, to the kind of life that happens outside the lunar dome of pregnancy and babyhood. Now my daughter slept through the night. I'd stopped nursing a week before the miscarriage, because when I was pregnant it had been so painful. My hips, the doctor had once said, would start to come together again once I was no longer nursing. My body would harden. I could do some sit-ups and probably get rid of the extra swell in my stomach. But the thought of it, the thought of going back to the world of harder bodies: it made me want to start crying again.

Thinking that, I glanced at my arm. The skin was older. I could see a mesh of very fine lines on my forearm. It had been so long since I'd scrutinized my arm: for so long, my body was for taking care of a baby. What did I care, then, about fine lines on my forearms? Now, however, now that I was having to put aside the idea of having another baby, perhaps having to put it aside for a year, perhaps forever, I realized I was reentering the world of contemplating my skin. Since the last time I had, my skin had gotten older. Looking down, I almost felt as though the skin of some older woman had been stitched onto my arms. I felt the way the monster does in the original film of *Frankenstein*, when, first coming to life, Boris Karloff looks at his hands with surprise and even wonder. Whose hands are these? he seems to be thinking. Whose skin is this that has been stitched onto my body?

Once, I remembered, I'd gone to a writer's residency and one of the old women there was working on an art project in which she took photographs of her skin and magnified them many times over, then pasted them on top of other images. All around her studio, there were photographs of oceans, trees, Greek statues, and ancient urns that—when you looked closer—had the wrinkled texture of her very old skin. In that moment of realization, something that had been extraordinarily beautiful—the bright, gleaming wrinkles on the skin of the ocean under the moon—suddenly became awful, and you realized what an absurd aversion you had to old skin.

I looked at Anna. She was staring out the front window of the car, as though in a trance, and I realized that, in addition to the smile lines around her eyes, the skin on her forehead was very dry. If I looked at it closely, in fact, her forehead seemed to be paper.

Years had passed since we'd gone to shows together in Austin. So many strange years, when both of us were trying to have children. Sitting there next to Anna, for the first time, I felt I could understand those women I'd occasionally seen while visiting my parents in recent years. Since those mudslides, my parents had sold their house in California; the constant threat of disasters had started to take their toll on my mother's well-being. Then, temporarily, they'd moved to a bungalow on a golf course, and that's where I'd visited them last, during a lull in the pandemic, the one time I'd felt it was safe to fly.

We'd put my daughter in her stroller and walked around the clubhouse so that my mother could point out women who had become addicted to face-lifts. It was the whole point of the walk; it was as though we'd gone birding. And some of these women really did look like they'd become other species. They were truly disfigured, with their puffy lips and their skin that seemed to be stretched too tightly over their bones.

"But you can do it well," my mother said. In her voice, there was a slight note of wonder: a childlike wonder; the wonder of a person coming to a new frontier. One of her friends, she told me, had gotten a very good face-lift.

We started to walk home. My mother was always beautiful. When I was young, she never wore makeup. She barely even brushed her hair. And even so, she was always beautiful, and she was always satisfied with her looks: no matter what else was uncertain in her life, she had a satisfaction with her looks that I found so reassuring, so it surprised me when it became clear that she was interested in this concept of face-lifts.

She told me that her friend—the one with the good face-lift—was in love with her new face. Then she told me that another friend had waited for years to get hers, and then finally did, only to learn, two months later, that she had terminal ovarian cancer.

"But you're not thinking of getting one," I said. "Are you?"

My mother laughed. "I don't know," she said. "But wouldn't it be nice to think you were getting a few more years out of your face?"

That night, I'd googled the process involved in face-lifts, and learned that, after administering a general anesthetic, the surgeon made a scalpel incision in the patient's face, beginning at the temple and then curving around the ear and ending again at the temple, through which they reached under the skin and redistributed the muscle and fat, then pulled back the skin a little more tightly before finally stitching it shut.

The idea of it had horrified me. In the morning, I'd told my mother she shouldn't ever get a face-lift. But now, looking down at the skin on my arm, which seemed to be the stitched-on skin of some other woman, I wondered whether the urge behind face-lifts was less to become beautiful and more to become one's own self again: the self you remembered, the last self you'd known. So that it would not be after the face-lift that you looked in the mirror and felt like Frankenstein's monster; no, that had been before, when you saw yourself with surprise and some wonder and thought: Whose face is this that has been stitched onto my body?

And is that, I wondered now, sitting beside Anna in her car, what Mary Shelley knew? What she learned in all those years of pregnancy? That we are all monsters, stitched together loosely, composed of remnants from other lives, pieces that often don't seem as though they could plausibly belong to us?

"She's fine," Anna was saying. She was looking out at the park, at the empty picnic pavilions, and there was a dazed tone in her voice. I remembered how cold I'd found her when I first met her in Austin: that slightly stoned manner she'd had, as though nothing were really affecting her. "Everything's okay," she said. "Everything's healthy."

# 20.

AND SO BEGAN that period of my life when I marked the passing weeks by HCG tests, and, between tests, went in to teach wearing my mask, no longer in space, no longer in the Arctic, no longer enclosed in those luminous days, but returned, back on Earth and the routines of earthly time, sorting, once again, through earthly numbers.

Often, walking to work, I made calculations: the chances of developing the kind of pregnancy I had developed were less than one in a thousand; the chances of the cancerous material returning and requiring chemotherapy were one in fifty; the chances of that kind of pregnancy recurring if you were to get pregnant again were closer to one in seventy; the chances were lower if you waited for a year, higher if you only waited six months, but about the same as six months if you waited for three.

At the same time, there were other calculations to make: the chances of my getting Covid at work; the chances of my giving it to my daughter; the chances of a young child getting seriously sick, chances that were, people reminded me at every possible moment, much less than the chances of her dying in an accident every time we got into the car. So then there were the chances of our getting into a car wreck. And the other common ways children have always been harmed, and the new ways for children to be harmed, new ways we've only recently invented: harm, for instance, as a result of global warming, breathing problems as a result of poor air quality, or violence as a result of the geopolitical shifts that will occur as more and more land becomes uninhabitable.

Life, I was aware, is a calculation of risk. And yet I couldn't help but long for that period in my life after the pandemic had begun when the three of us had stayed home. We had no reason to leave the house in the car. We were safe within the confines of our little existence.

I missed that time. In my office, I didn't change the calendar from March 2020. I left the bags for breast milk in my drawer. I left them there like hexes or charms, as though they might remind the universe to intervene once again and send me and my daughter back home, back to that safer and more solitary planet.

One night in September, I sent a few emails before bed, and then made the mistake of checking the news: an unprecedented storm flooding Texas; the Taliban banning girls from going to school; Amy Coney Barrett defending the Supreme Court's decision to uphold the Texas law allowing citizens to sue one another to stop abortions after six weeks.

Then I went to sleep. That night, I woke around two and began thinking about the risk I was exposing my daughter to by returning to teaching. I wondered about what kind of mask I should wear. I wondered about her beloved babysitter, an extraordinarily mature and responsible young woman, but a college student nevertheless, who came to look after her while I was at school. What kind of mask should she wear? Should I buy her the same expensive masks I was thinking of getting myself? Lying there in the darkness, trying to calculate risk, thinking about the possibility of my daughter ending up in the hospital, I wasn't crying, but for some reason tears began to fall down my face. I sat up and reached for the dog. For a while, he let me hold him: both of our heads were on my pillow. His stomach was so velvety. How many anxious nights had he let me hold him, here, but also in Montana and New York and Texas? All those places I lived before I came here.

After a while, however, he gently struggled out of my arms and returned to the end of the bed. The tears had stopped, but I couldn't sleep. Finally, I got up. I went downstairs. Outside, the moon was full. Around it, there was a halo of silver. I thought of the glorious, pink sunset in Texas when I visited Anna: the result, she had told me, of the El Dorado fires, caused by a couple's gender reveal.

Now, to compound the tragedy—since we can't, it seems, live with tragedy unless we add another—the state of California had charged them with manslaughter. They'd been in jail for months, since they hadn't made bail. Who knew what was happening to their little baby, whose gender they'd announced with such anticipation?

Last summer: that baby was still safe in her mother's belly. My baby still wasn't sleeping through the night. I was preparing for a semester online, and right before school started, the derecho had swept through Iowa City, felling half the trees on our street. Even now, they were still removing the damaged trees. Total Care Company was the outfit that came to take them away; they were in our neighborhood with their cranes every day. The other afternoon, I'd watched them cut down a limb the size of an oak tree. They used the crane to carry it over our neighbor's rooftop, and now, in our backyard, there were two new swathes of emptiness through which to see the moon, and the medevac helicopters coming and going from the hospital.

I was standing there at the window, looking up at the gaps in the treetops while the sky behind them became paler, when I heard a quiet knock on the door. I thought I'd imagined it. Then I heard another. I went to check, and when I opened the door, I saw Anna.

"I'm sorry," she said.

I stared at her. Her face was white as a second moon in the darkness, her belly swelling slightly under a raincoat.

"I'm really sorry," she said. "I told myself I'd just drive by, but then I saw the light."

I didn't know what to say. She was just standing there in front of the door, with her hands hanging by her sides, looking a little bit startled, as though I were the one who had surprised her.

"I'm sorry," she said again, and for some reason I leaned forward to hug her, and she started crying.


WE SAT ON the front porch, next to the hydrangeas, their blooms soft and pale in the darkness, while she told me the whole story, and, like Walton, I prepared to record it.

She'd come, she said, to Iowa with her frozen, unviable embryos, because Iowa gave her a lab of her own. She'd used the same service they used to transport frozen mouse embryos to transport her own embryos from the clinic. It had all been strangely easy, a matter of some paperwork. The grant she'd received gave her basically unlimited funds. She was meant to study ways of engineering embryos to be Covid resistant. She had declined the offer of assistants.

In her new lab, without anyone to bother her, she'd used CRISPR gene editing to revise her embryos. She hadn't, not at first, tried to make any changes beyond the gene sequence that caused unviability. She had not, for instance, tried to make them immune to any of the diseases that threaten children.

Even so, she said, she did not delude herself into thinking that she was not overreaching. How far she'd ventured beyond the "natural." But at the same time: she couldn't be sure how many of the problems in her embryos were a result of the IVF process. Errors in the way embryos are frozen can cause aneuploidies. So can the stress of genetic testing, and excessive follicular stimulation of the kind we use to harvest eggs. So can the culture media and incubators we use to develop embryos, which must be carefully monitored by human technicians, and any failure on their part can lead to unviable aneuploidy in an embryo that, otherwise, would have been healthy.

So how many of these aneuploidies, Anna wanted to know, were actually "natural"? And furthermore, she said, even if you're not taking into account the potential harm we do in the IVF process, how many of our eggs, which would have otherwise been viable, become nonviable because of exposure to plastics and pesticides and poor air quality, especially poor air quality related to smoke from forest fires? How many of our sperm? There's no such thing, Anna told me, as a natural embryo anymore, and, having convinced herself of this fact, she'd set to work in her lab: altering nonviable embryos into viable embryos she could implant in herself.

Once she got to work, she said, she felt as though what she was doing was perfectly right. She felt, she told me, that she was only returning her embryos to their "natural" state, the state they'd have been in if they'd been conceived in a world without pollution and global warming. As she had continued to work, she told me, she had begun to feel great sympathy with people who protest abortion, people who believe that babies should be allowed to develop naturally. That had been precisely what she'd felt while she was employing CRISPR in her lab: that these babies should be allowed to develop naturally. Miracles that they were, they should be allowed to survive, as they would have been if we hadn't so horribly engineered our environment to be dangerous to growing embryos and also to the women who carry them.

She had, therefore, introduced healthy genes where the risk-carrying genes had been before, and then she'd realized that it would be immoral not to also alter her embryo's genes in ways that would protect them from man-made disaster: pandemic, for instance, the effects of global warming, the risks involved with restricted abortion access. And so she'd also altered the genes that would make her embryos susceptible to Covid and the flu, genes that would make them susceptible to asthma, to hemorrhage and preeclampsia.

Then, finally, she'd purchased a new set of implantation tools, human tools, larger than the ones she used to implant embryos in her mice. Everything was larger, but it was the same technology: the speculum, the ultrasound machine that guided the catheter into the uterus. Using the image on the machine to guide her hand, she'd been able to do it herself. Once again, she'd been surprised by how easy it was: it was as though, her whole life, she'd been practicing for this.

At first, when it worked, and when the pregnancy stuck, she'd been euphoric. But as time passed, time in which she wasn't caught up in the frenzy of accomplishing what she'd set out to accomplish, she had started to worry. The truth was that she couldn't be perfectly certain that the embryo she'd implanted was healthy. She was confident in her techniques. She knew she'd done a better job than someone like He Jiankui, and of course she'd run all the standard tests.

But then all researchers were confident. Frankenstein was confident, in those last days before his creature came to life. You have to be confident, she said, to be a researcher. But recent studies showed that in experimental embryonic modifications on test animals, there was a 16 percent rate of accidental mutation that couldn't be picked up by standard tests.

So there was a 16 percent chance, Anna told me, that in fixing the lethal genes, she'd introduced a new mutation, a mutation so new that it couldn't be picked up by standard tests, which meant that it was impossible to know how severe the results of the mutations might be. Maybe—probably—they'd be perfectly harmless. But maybe they'd cause some devastating problem, antibiotic resistance, or a fatal disease.

What if, Anna asked me, while the globes of the hydrangea blooms bobbed around us like multiple moons, my daughter has an abnormally long tongue like those rabbits, who starved to death because they couldn't eat? What if she has wings?

"But wouldn't you know?" I asked Anna. "Wouldn't you have seen it on the ultrasounds?"

Anna shook her head. She'd stopped crying. She was holding her knees with her arms, and now, once again, everything she said was flat. No, no, she said. She hadn't gone in for any scans. She was too scared. What if something was wrong? What if they realized what she'd done? What if, like He Jiankui, they put her in prison? Then what would happen to her baby?

"But how would they know that you were the one who interfered?" I asked. "Couldn't those mutations just have been another tragic accident? The result of exposure to pesticides, or toxins, or just the random lethal way of the universe?"

"But if it's something they've never seen," Anna said. Then she looked at me. "If it's something that's clearly out of the ordinary? I just—I need you to come with me."

I stared at her. "For what?"

"There's an ultrasound machine in my department," she said. "We use it on the animals."

"You're going to give yourself an ultrasound?"

"Yes," she said. "You were there with me last time. Last time, I couldn't have done it without you. Please. Please come with me again."

# 21.

ENTERING THE HOSPITAL at night was like entering a university library during the summer: the silence, the squeaking of linoleum floors. The automatic lights that flickered on a few moments after we had been standing in darkness.

For a moment, I thought of the floor of the library where I'd often studied when I was a graduate student in Texas: that moment of waiting for the lights to flicker on, at which point you could begin to move toward your row in the stacks, following the numbers, keeping in mind to avoid the corner where, several years before, the shooter who ran through the halls of the English building firing rounds into classrooms had retreated to shoot himself in the head. In that corner, there was still a stubborn bloodstain in the blue carpet that was best avoided when you looked for your books.

Now I was following Anna down another hall lit by flickering lights, and into a lab, where we were surrounded by the hulking shapes of the centrifuges, freezers, animal cages, and, in another, smaller office, the sonogram machine.

There was no patient chair, as there had been when I had my sonograms. This time, there was only a large table, a desk, and an office chair, and this is where Anna sat after she'd bent over the machine, fumbling with the buttons.

I stood beside her. The screen over the machine blinked on. I realized I was getting hot. From the other room, I could hear the mice squeaking. I was a curse on these machines. My vision began to swim. It seemed clear to me that my presence would cause things to go badly. I was getting hotter and hotter, and as Anna lifted her shirt and prepared to begin rolling the knob over her belly, I suddenly felt as though I might faint. What if what we found was emptiness? Or what if we found something else?

Then I propped myself against the table, and Anna reached for my hand. With one hand, she held on to me, and with the other she rolled the knob over her belly. I gripped her hand and, because I didn't want to look at her, I kept my eyes trained on the screen, where the darkness became lighter, and then the crackling gray and white of a picture: the moonscape I recognized, the inside of a womb. The white and gray caves and cliffs, the dark absences of the ovaries, the sloping sides of the uterus, and there the baby: curled in its fetal shape, nestled with its forehead pressed against the placenta.

Her heart whooshed. Her chest stretched. Then she wriggled. With such grace it took my breath away, she somersaulted and kicked. I laughed. It was such a relief. There she was: somersaulting and kicking and playing in that cave on the moon where there was no gravity, where she was perfectly light.

She seemed to be showing off. This is how easy it is, she seemed to say. This is how free I am, living my life.

Anna was laughing as well. She was laughing at the same time she was crying, while her baby showed off her somersaults. After a while, I held the knob on Anna's belly while Anna used the keyboard to make calculations. Ten fingers, ten toes. Two ears, two arms, and two legs. A nose. A bladder that filled. Spine length, femur length, nuchal folds.

"No wings," Anna said.

"Not even one," I said.

"No fins."

"A shame. She could have used those fins in the floods."

Anna laughed. She had stopped measuring. Now she was just looking up at the screen: the cliffs, the recesses, the dark pools, and the baby flipping one more time.

"She likes it in there."

I nodded. "She's happy."

"You almost wish she could stay in there forever."

"She'll be happy here also," I said, and Anna nodded, though of course we both knew there was no guarantee, that it was a difficult world, and that all Anna could do was try in the best way she could to take care of this creature.

# 22.

WHEN ANNA DROPPED me off, it was nearly light. I made myself coffee, then heard the dog coming down the stairs to sit with me. On the couch, we sat together, his head on my knee, until I heard the sounds of my baby waking.

As though nothing out of the usual had occurred, the weeks went on. Teaching was fine. My students and I settled into a routine, just as I'd settled into the routine of going into the hospital for my weekly tests and doing what I could not to get pregnant.

There was, through it all, the odd feeling of stillness. There was the feeling of suspension, or perhaps it would be more accurate to say there was the feeling of time having been turned off, time, for me, having come to be associated with weeks and months of trying to have a baby.

Only my daughter was changing. She was saying new words every day: "dunder" and "flower," "breakfast" and "acorn." The clothes I'd bought her last spring—clothes that were once long and loose—were now tighter and shorter, and she'd grown out of her summer shoes, and that's what I was doing—searching online for fall shoes for toddlers, instead of working on the novel I should have been writing—when Anna called me.

She was moving to Boston. BU had offered her a lab, and a promotion, and better money—the Covid research money, she told me, was still liberally flowing—and she felt it would be nice to afford a bigger house for the baby. She'd visited last week. She'd had an appointment with the doctor she was planning to see there. Everything had gone fine: all was well, apparently, with the baby.

That weekend, her last weekend, we met in the park to go on a walk. That morning, I'd woken early, and from the window in my office, while I worked on a talk I was meant to give at a conference on space travel in science fiction, I watched the full moon fall down into the trees, and then a pink and purple light rise up between the black branches. Then the whole sky was sage green, and the tops of the trees were blowing left and right.

A thunderstorm: how strange. My phone hadn't predicted it. Stray leaves were getting tossed over the treetops. By the time the rest of the house woke, the sky had grown black again and it had started to thunder. I took the dog out for a walk before the rain started falling. Flashes of lightning occasionally turned the world yellow. The world was black and white and yellow, like the world in an old film, like the night when the movie version of Frankenstein's creature came to life. The dog was scared, so we turned around and went home. Just as we got to the door, the rain started to fall.

For a while, I went upstairs and played with my husband and my daughter. We were in her room. Outside, the sky was black, shot through with occasional lightning. Rain drummed on the roof. The dog was cowering in my husband's arms. My daughter was playing happily, occasionally looking up to sing, "Dunder!"

I laughed. She was so joyful. It was a joyful version of that night in the movie when the creature comes to life. Or so I thought, and then I realized: Perhaps this is the novel to write. A novel about a woman Walton and a woman Frankenstein, and their ambitions to bring a creature to life.

It would be a novel about creatures, I thought, but the novel, too, would also be a creature. It would be made of disparate parts, flesh and bone, blood lost in a hemorrhage, stitched-together old skin. A book that would stir with uneasy life. A little disjointed, perhaps, but a book I wouldn't leave. A book I'd keep and tend until it was ready to go on without me.

Maybe it could work. I thought about it for a while, and helped my daughter build a tower with blocks, and when we were done, I stood and stretched and realized it had stopped raining. In an instant, the clouds had broken up and the light had come back, and the drops of rain on the windows were gleaming. Everything was bright and clean: the whole world had been made new again.

When I went outside to drive to the park to see Anna, I realized it was fall. The storm had scrubbed away what was left of the summer. In a few weeks, my daughter would turn two; then she'd start day care. She'd leave the small circle of our house, the walks we took in our neighborhood.

As I drove, I looked around. This was the world my daughter would live in. The leaves on the elm trees that lined River Street—leaves from the trees that had survived the derecho—had turned a brilliant yellow, and now, gently, in the slight wind left from the storm, they were eddying down. Some had fallen on the river, and, as I crossed the bridge, I could see them sailing away: vast fleets of little bright boats.

I slowed as I crossed the river. I rolled the window down. How beautiful that river was, through the window of my car. The fine wrinkles of its skin had caught the gold light of the sun; the wind passed over it, and the water beneath it. That river was beautiful because it was old. It was beautiful because of what it had carried, because of what had slipped through it. If you thought of it as separate, somehow, from the water that passed through on its way to the ocean, then really the river was nothing at all, or something massive, something massively powerful because it wasn't full: because it was empty enough to carry that water.

I loved that river. Polluted as it was, I loved that river so much. I loved the sycamore trees that lined the path along it, their leaves brown now, their bark in tatters. This earth's the right home for me, I thought to myself, probably misquoting a poem I couldn't quite place. But it pleased me to think it: This earth's the right home for me. I am, I thought, a creature of these trees and this water.

Or so I said to myself, and it felt true, and I kept the window down as I rolled on along the winding streets that led to the park, the wind, full of the sweetness of decaying leaves and cold water, rushing past my face, making me feel hollow and passed through, alive in every empty bone of my body.

At the park, Anna was waiting for me at a picnic bench under a maple tree, its leaves shockingly gold and shading to red, so that, from a distance, shone through by the sun, the trees seemed to be coral. When I came closer to her, I was surprised to see that she'd gotten more visibly pregnant through all those weeks when, for me, time had seemed to slow to a halt.

The closer I got to her, the more distant she seemed: as though I was watching a movie in which she was a character. There she was, sitting under that glowing tree, so hopeful, so young, and so pretty. Her pregnancy, it seemed to me, had erased all that had come before: her life in Texas, those tortured years she'd spent with her ex-boyfriend. It had erased the way her colleague had broken up with her, the years she'd tried to find a new partner, and the years when she'd given up, when she'd tried and failed to get pregnant.

Her pregnancy had released her from all that. It had allowed her to set sail, it would give her a chance to start afresh on a new planet. That's where she was heading. Even as I walked toward her, and hugged her, and even as we set off down the trail, in the bright clear sunshine of autumn, with the leaves twisting down all around us, the goldenrod bright in the restored prairie, the sweet sound of the creek that was still running, I felt that she was departing.

I missed her already. In my mind, I wished her a safe journey. For a moment, in the bright, clear sunshine of autumn on Earth, autumn on this failing and outrageously beautiful planet, she stopped walking and said something to me. Beyond her, the glowing pink leaves of a serviceberry tree. Then Anna laughed, and she was moving again: moving off toward her car, her and her little baby.

I waved. I wished her well. I felt as though I should throw rice. There she was: a character whose revolving door had swung into the light. She opened the door of her car. It was a ship. She stepped into her ship, and she and her daughter sailed away from the park and into the airy distance.

I stood there and watched them set off: out of the parking lot, and down the long driveway that threaded past the cemetery. The gold leaves drifted around me, each one edged with crimson. Everything was fading, yes, we had come to the end, but the air smelled like apples. The blue sky was shining.

And then they were gone, and I was alone. For a moment, I felt a slight chill. Then I looked around: the gold leaves, the blue sky, the gravestones in the cemetery. This was, I thought again, the planet for me.

I had come home, I thought, from the Arctic. I had come back from the moon. There would be new responsibilities: the small responsibilities of tending a home, the small responsibilities of growing old in a troubled place. But now I would stay. Watching Anna sail off, I waved. I waved to her from the shore of my own, finally returned-to home country.

# Acknowledgments

ALL MY THANKS TO GABRIELLA DOOB, HELEN ATSMA, MIRIAM Parker, and everyone at Ecco; Sophie Missing and everyone at Scribner UK; Susanna Lea, Kerry Glencorse, Mark Kessler, and everyone at Susanna Lea Associates; the English departments at the University of Iowa and Montana State University; my students; the T. S. Eliot Foundation; Louisa Thomas, Karen Olsson, and Cecily Parks; Hannah Moore; my family, and especially William Callahan.